"I'm here to study, Piers. No messing about."

Piers's sudden kiss had left Annabel furious with her own uncontrolled reaction.

"So elegantly put! And so difficult to comply with. I can't promise never to be tempted." Piers's dark eyes explored her flushed face and lips. "I had just a fleeting impression that we were of one mind about this little experience."

"You took me completely by surprise!" Annabel protested.

"Was that it?" Piers teased. "But I thought a woman of the eighties was ready for anything."

"I think you'd better go, please," Annabel responded tightly.

"I'm going," Piers said, chuckling. "And I'm going to enjoy working with you. Don't ever calm down too much, will you?"

Calm down, Annabel fumed. How ironic that the last man she wanted to be kissed by should be the first to have such an effect!

Alison York is a new writer in the Harlequin Romance line. The fast-paced style of her writing and lively, well-developed characters as evidenced in this first novel will have readers eagerly awaiting her second appearance in print.

No Sad Song
Alison York

Harlequin Books

TORONTO • NEW YORK • LONDON
AMSTERDAM • PARIS • SYDNEY • HAMBURG
STOCKHOLM • ATHENS • TOKYO • MILAN

Original hardcover edition published in 1987
by Mills & Boon Limited

ISBN 0-373-02880-6

Harlequin Romance first edition December 1987

CHAPTER ONE

'ANNABEL?'

The slight, dark girl, on her knees sorting out the music someone had left in an unholy shambles in the stockroom, looked up at the sound of her name.

'Yes?'

The second-year student who had put his head round the door stepped inside with an exaggerated groan.

'Trust you to be in the last place I've looked! I've scoured the college from top to bottom . . . every recital hall and rehearsal room . . . even the women's loos, heaven help me!'

Annabel Foley pushed back her mop of dark hair with one dusty hand and blinked as a shaft of late afternoon sunshine dazzled her grey eyes.

'You're lucky to find me at all. I could be gone for good by now. What's so urgent?'

'Moore wants to speak to you—said he knew you were coming in today some time to return books or whatever. He's in his office. You'd better hurry, he looked even wilder than usual.'

Annabel sighed at the mention of the Senior Vocal Studies Tutor's name.

'Oh God! Thanks, anyway. I'll go straight up.' She shuffled the last pile of scores into tidiness and put them back on the shelf.

No doubt she was in for another in-depth analysis of last night. Each summer the final year students staged an end-of-term production in the local repertory theatre. This year it had been *The Marriage of Figaro*, and as she sang the coveted role of the Countess, Annabel had had a glorious foretaste of what her future could be like—given, it had to be conceded, mega-doses of both good luck and hard work.

What a pity she hadn't gone straight home to Oxford after the performance, she thought now. With applause ringing in her ears she would have had some sense of achievement to crown her three years at the School of Music. Instead, her crowd had elected to stay on for a last night out together at Gino's, their favourite night spot when they could afford it, which wasn't often. It would probably be more of a wake than a celebration, and now she was in line for one of Francis Moore's famous post-mortems. He would discuss the rights and wrongs of every semi-quaver she had sung, and send her off to join the rat-race with her self-confidence battered down to zero level.

Grubbing around in the stockroom had done nothing for her shirt, which, at this stage of term, hadn't been freshly laundered in any case. She slapped at the dusty streaks to no avail. Oh, what the hell? He would have to take her as she was. Moore wouldn't even notice unless she had a treble clef stamped on her front, anyway.

From the end of the second-floor corridor she could hear his voice three rooms along, rising and falling with its usual ebullience. She assumed he was on the phone, but as she tapped on the partly open door it swung back a little, and she saw through the gap that someone was in there with him.

It was no one she knew. He was half-sitting on the desk, his dark, poised stillness in eloquent contrast to Francis Moore's excited gesticulations. A slight nod punctuated the torrent of words directed at him now and then, and a raised eyebrow seemed to serve when dissent was called for.

A bit of a smoothie, Annabel thought, wishing she had seen him before knocking, but it was too late to draw back now. He turned narrow, dark, intelligent eyes on her, raising both eyebrows at the sight of her, and at the same time Francis Moore snatched the door fully open.

'Ah, here you are at last! Come along in. This——' He broke off with an exclamation of annoyance as the telephone trilled. 'Confounded thing—never stops! Do excuse me.' He snatched up the receiver, and after an irritable, 'Yes. Moore here,' he became involved in conversation.

Annabel moved into the room with a brief smile at the stranger, and stood waiting, trying not to look aware of the steady inspection she was undergoing. It wasn't just her shirt, she thought uncomfortably. Last night she had been so tired after the performance that she had showered off the dust of the theatre and put a towel over the pillow, leaving her hair to dry as it would. This morning she had been too busy packing to deal with it, and it was now a totally undisciplined curly mass, waiting to be hot-brushed into order before tonight's farewell party.

The man whose dark eyes had only just finished their slow survey of her was, on the other hand, immaculately groomed and elegantly dressed in black shirt and trousers, his grey tie spiked by an opal pin, a gunmetal grey leather jacket slung casually from his shoulders.

'Sorry about that.' Francis Moore replaced the receiver and rubbed his hands together officiously. 'Now, I'm afraid I must dash downstairs and deal with the problem that's just arisen.' He seemed to have forgotten that Annabel was there. 'If I bring the car round to the front entrance in, say, a quarter of an hour, will that be all right? Does it give you long enough?' he asked the stranger.

'Surely.' The voice was as dark as the person. It was deep and incisive, and the rather affected choice of word confirmed Annabel's first impression. Definitely a poseur.

She looked helplessly at the door as it closed behind her tutor, then at the man, who stood up and indicated the chair beside her.

'Do sit down, Miss Foley.' He at least had some idea of who she was, then. He remained standing, quite relaxed, looking down at her.

'I would have liked to speak to you after the performance last night,' he went on, 'but I had guests with me and we'd arranged to go on to supper afterwards.'

'Yes, of course.' A silly reply, but what else could she say? Annabel thought irritably. She was slightly piqued that he hadn't said he had enjoyed the performance, just that he had been there.

But he wasn't really concerned with her reply. He was totally absorbed in his own thoughts, which he now made known.

'You really should practise more relaxation before you go on stage. Release the back of the tongue ... open the throat ... You must surely have been taught how to do all this? There was restriction in your voice and enunciation for almost the whole of the first aria. It shouldn't happen.'

'I was nervous at that point. Who wouldn't be?' The protest was stung out of her by the unexpected outspokenness of his comments.

'Nerves have to be dealt with.' Almost without drawing breath, he embarked on a dissection of her performance that stunned her with its calm clinical objectiveness.

Note by note, word by word, movement by movement, he took apart every act of the opera while she sat there in mounting anger and frustration. Who was he to speak to her like this? Moore was one thing, but no complete stranger should feel free to give such uninhibited criticism.

'The audience seemed satisfied enough with the perform-ance,' she broke in at last rather sharply.

He shrugged. 'A provincial audience is bound to be less critical than the average London one, I suppose.'

Annabel stiffened. 'Musical appreciation doesn't fade out completely beyond commuting distance of Covent Garden, you know!'

'But it is somewhat suspect in an audience consisting largely of friends and relatives of the performers, don't you think?'

For a moment their eyes locked, his mildly amused, Annabel's glittering with a mixture of annoyance and painful acknowledgement of the unwelcome fact that what he said was right.

He had criticised harshly, but she was forced to recognise the professional accuracy behind his comments. Last night she had lapped up the praise and applause—who wouldn't?—but she knew her weak spots better than anyone. That, however, did not make it acceptable to have them probed by someone who just happened to be in Moore's office at the same time as herself.

She decided to return fire. 'I'm afraid I haven't the least idea who you are. I presume you . . . dabble in opera too?' She liked the 'dabble'. Let him have a sample of being cut down to size as well!

'Didn't Francis tell you? Typical of the man.' He felt in

the inside pocket of his jacket and took out a card. 'This should clarify matters.'

She took it from him, thinking scornfully that yes, such a man would have gilt edges on his card, and glanced at the name with studied carelessness.

She was totally unprepared for the way the small print suddenly danced before her eyes, then zoomed crazily away into a grey blur as her mind tried to reject the words formed by the italic lettering. The wounding nature of his criticism faded away into insignificance beside the horrible fact that it was Piers Bellingham who had made it: Piers Bellingham, the agent responsible for what had happened to Kate. Annabel realised that she was shivering. It was eighteen months ago now, and for much of the time she didn't think of Kate at all—so much at least had she progressed since that nightmare time in her second year at college. But when she did remember her vivid, laughing friend, there was always this sickening jolt, then the fight to convince herself all over again that Kate was truly dead.

She stared fixedly at the hated name, struggling to control herself while he leaned against the desk waiting for—what? Admiration? A gasp of humble thankfulness that such a high flier as he should give her the benefit of his opinions? Certainly not for the hot stream of vituperation that she could feel rising in her.

'Advice from a top agent. I see . . .' she said eventually.

He misread her reaction as wounded pride.

'You mustn't take what I said too much to heart.'

His patronising tone galvanised her into standing up and preparing to leave. 'I won't,' she replied briefly.

He restrained her with one lean, long-fingered hand.

Annabel looked down at it as though a snake rested on her arm.

'To head, yes. But not to heart,' he emphasised.

She didn't look at him. 'I shall remember. And now I think you must have said it all?' She tried to move past him to the door as she spoke, but the hard fingers tightened on her arm.

'Indeed I have not. I've barely started. I was leading up—perhaps in a somewhat roundabout way—to an offer to represent you.'

Sheer incredulity made her stare up into his face then, in time to catch the quickly smothered start of a smile— whether superior, mocking or patronising there was no time to judge. How could Moore have let her in for this meeting with the man who had destroyed Kate? she thought passionately. Had he no sensitivity at all? Revulsion that Piers Bellingham should dare to suggest himself as her agent after all she knew about him brought a quick answer to her lips.

'Surely you're not a man to take up lost causes, Mr Bellingham?'

The dark eyes widened slightly in mocking surprise. 'And surely you don't think of yourself as a lost cause— though, indeed, it's true that I wouldn't have the slightest desire to represent you if you were. You have a beautiful voice ... most moving ... but inexperienced. The experience I can provide.'

A sharp mental picture of the 'experience' that had led to Kate's death blazed in Annabel's mind.

'I don't doubt that you can provide experience of all kinds,' she said coldly, 'but I already happen to be registered with an agent.' The small triumph implicit in the words gave an unconsciously proud lift to her head.

'May I ask which one?'

'Douglas Ryman. He approached me after the mid-year recital in the Town Hall, and I gladly accepted his offer.'

'I see. A local man.'

Her control slipped again at the condescension in his words. 'He's good and straight—and that's everyone's opinion. I ask no more of an agent.'

His reply rapped back at her. 'An agent can be good and straight. He can also be of significance.'

'And not over-endowed with modesty.' She shouldn't have said that, but she was surprised to see that this time his smile seemed genuine and stayed there, even extending as far as a gleam in the so far inscrutable brown eyes.

'I'm realistic. I know people. I have contacts that Doug Ryman can only dream about. Ask him. He's man enough to tell you where your best interests lie ... which could be one reason, sadly, why he's where *he* is instead of where *I* am.'

'In my book loyalty ranks higher than ambition,' said Annabel, putting his card down on the desk by his side with a satisfying little click. 'So it's a case of thanks, but no thanks, Mr Bellingham. And now, I'm sure Mr Moore will be risking a parking ticket waiting for you.'

As he stood upright, she realised with a brief flash of ridiculous alarm how tall he was, and that his lazily relaxed appearance was deceptive.

'Think about it,' he said, his voice authoritative and compelling. 'It's your career.'

Annabel tore her eyes away from the demand in his and turned to leave the office without another word, shaken by his insistence. The man exuded a sense of single-mindedness that was frightening in its intensity. Now that she had met him, she could come somewhere near understanding the effect he'd had on Kate. If one brief meeting could be so disturbing, how much more shattering must it have been to be taken and moulded to his will over weeks and months.

Damn him! She squeezed her eyes to fight back the sudden threat of tears. The end of college had her emotional enough already ... and now he'd conjured up such memories of Kate with all their attendant sadness.

'Annabel! Are you off? I'm going to miss you.' She had almost bumped into the first-year girl she had been twinned with this year under the college's system of linking first and final year students for the help of the former.

Annabel returned the girl's hug and promised to keep in touch. Jane Bowman had given nothing like the amount of trouble she herself had caused Kate, her own 'twin' in her first year, she thought as she went out into town on her way home.

Kate ... There had been something so special about her—a warmth of personality and generosity of spirit that enhanced and transcended the talent she undoubtedly had and which Piers Bellingham had been quick to recognise and exploit.

Annabel had suffered badly from homesickness and strangeness in her early days at college. It was Kate who had sensed the unease beneath the cool, self-possessed-seeming outer shell, and she who had dispelled the depression with cups of coffee and understanding though never indulgent chats at all hours. It was thanks to her that Annabel had stayed the course, for she had been on the point of walking out at the end of the first term.

It was hard to realise now what a state she had been in—

and all over a man who, seen in retrospect, was harmlessness itself.

Marc Gerard, one of the group of foreign language assistants needed by the opera students, had fallen for her in a big, Gallic way. He was little past student age himself, and, being French, had not hesitated to make a series of enthusiastic passes at her in the one-to-one conversation sessions.

Annabel, not the least bit attracted to him and still fresh from school where staff and pupils kept their distance, had not known how to handle the situation.

With the end-of-term exams looming, everything suddenly got out of proportion. One day, after a particularly intense early session with him, she had gone rushing hysterically to Kate's room. She was going to pack everything in and leave that very morning. She couldn't face the man and his wandering hands and incomprehensible mutterings any longer.

Kate's reaction was typically calm and sensible.

'Tell him where he gets off!' she said placidly. 'That's all that's needed. Your "confused maiden" act only spurs him on.'

'But he's a member of *staff*. How can I?' Annabel wailed.

'He's a pain. Just tell him so in simple English. He'll get the point.' Then, seeing that Annabel really was at the end of her tether and quite beyond joking, Kate flung down her bag and pulled her into her room.

'You really mean it, don't you? Come in, love. Sit down and I'll put the kettle on'

It was only a couple of hours and several cups of coffee later that Annabel, talked into sanity again, discovered to her horror that Kate had cut an exam to help her through the crisis.

It all worked out in the end. Francis Moore, shocked to learn that one of his star pupils should so jeopardise her chances of success, had made Kate stay in his study when the affair was explained to him so that she had no chance of contact with the other students of her year. Then he moved heaven and earth throughout the department to get permission for her to sit the exam during the lunch hour.

But Kate had not known that would happen. Her readiness to help had been generous and totally selfless. That was the exceptional kind of person she was . . . and the kind Piers Bellingham had destroyed.

Annabel had been so immersed in thoughts of the past that she was back at the tiny flat she shared with Wendy James, another final year student, before she realised it. The inner city area where they lived was a mixture of commercial premises and run-down, finely proportioned Victorian houses, relics of the days before the town grew and spread to swallow them up in its heart.

Their place was over a furniture shop, its pokiness compensated for by the fact that there were no downstairs neighbours to disturb or be disturbed by.

Wendy was home, busy turning the tail end of a bag of chips into a disgusting-looking sandwich.

'Hi. Thought you were going straight in and out again. You've been quite a time,' she said.

'That was the idea, but Moore wanted to see me.' Annabel told Wendy briefly what had happened, and saw, as she had expected, the blue eyes widen and the nice, plump face register that Wendy was impressed. Very impressed.

'Don't get too excited,' she added shortly. 'I turned him down.'

'You *what?*' Wendy gave a squeal of outrage. 'Oh, Annabel! You've got to be mad!'

Annabel could see well enough how it must look to Wendy, who so far had neither work nor agent in prospect.

'I couldn't get involved with him of all people, Wendy,' she said. 'Apart from the fact that I've already signed up with Doug Ryman, there's Kate.'

Wendy looked dumbfounded. 'What about Kate? What has she to do with anything?'

'Surely you remember that he managed her . . . and that she died?' Annabel's voice trembled on the words. 'How can everybody forget so completely?'

'But Kate had an accident. What on earth has that to do with you, *now?* If Piers Bellingham had asked me to go on his books, I'd accept like a shot, I can tell you.'

Kate was just another unfortunate statistic to most people now, Annabel thought painfully. But of course, to give Wendy credit, she had never had reason to suspect that there was more to Kate's death than the newspapers had revealed.

'Maybe the pace that was too much for Kate would be too much for me,' she said slowly. 'That's when accidents happen . . . when people are tired out.' Or when they're lonely or heartbroken, as she had known from one of Kate's letters that her friend was.

'But you're not like that!' Wendy insisted hotly. 'You thrive on work. It's food and drink to you. Oh, Annabel! Think how many people get killed crossing the road. You don't stay rooted to the spot because of that.'

It was no use arguing. 'I wish I hadn't told you,' Annabel

said. 'I can't expect you to see it as I do, I suppose. But that's the way it is. Over. Settled. My agent is Doug Ryman.'

'A Midlands man.' Wendy had hit on the same note of criticism as Piers Bellingham.

'You thought he was good enough before!' Annabel said sharply.

'That was *before*. To me, yes. He'd be the crumb I'd snatch at and be thankful. But you've been offered the ruddy cake! Annabel, I repeat—you're crazy.'

'Let's forget it. I'm going to do something about my hair now, and have a bath if you've had yours. Is that all right?'

Wendy nodded. 'I've got a hundred and one errands to take care of—including going round to Zak's to return his squash racquet. So I'll probably leave before you do and meet you at Gino's.'

'Fine. And Wendy—don't tell anyone else about Piers Bellingham, will you? Promise?'

'So you do realise how daft you are?' rang in Annabel's ears as she closed her bedroom door behind her.

It was hopeless expecting any of the others to understand just how she felt. To her knowledge, not one of them knew anything of the trouble that had led, if not directly to Kate's death, certainly to the state of mind that had made her so fatally uncaring of her own safety.

If only I knew what happened, Annabel thought unhappily as she undressed and stuffed her discarded clothes into the open suitcase over which she had to step each time she crossed the tiny bedroom. For once she was quite unaware of the inconvenience. She was on automatic pilot as she pinned up her hair and filled the bath. Kate Elston haunted her.

Two years ago when Kate had announced that Piers
Bellingham wanted to represent her, the news went round
college on a wave of excitement and speculation. He was
known to be far more than just a run-of-the-mill agent. He
was making his name as someone who could spot a winner
in the musical stakes, and his hothouse forcing methods of
organising training and performances were both criticised
and reluctantly admired.

Like Jane tonight, Annabel had begged Kate to write to
her, and over the months she had received two letters. The
first was full of delighted enthusiasm. Kate loved London.
Recital venues known and unknown to Annabel sprinkled
the letter. St Giles, Cripplegate . . . St John's, Smith Square
. . . the Purcell Room . . . the Wigmore Hall . . . the Queen
Elizabeth Hall.

But it was not all work, Kate had implied somewhat
mysteriously. Life was exciting for other reasons that she
could only hint at so far. The fact that Piers Bellingham's
name featured a lot made it easy for Annabel to put two
and two together. The involvement between singer and
agent was, it seemed, developing into something more.

There were one or two references to Kate in the press
which Annabel cut out and kept, but as her second year got
into its swing her own busy life inevitably pushed Kate into
the background.

The second letter came just before the end of term when
the Christmas concert was taking up all Annabel's time and
thoughts. She was producing it, and she wanted desperately
for it to be good.

It was a confused and disturbing letter. Kate's writing
had changed from the familiar flamboyant forward-
sloping script to a wandering scrawl it was hard to

decipher. She complained pathetically but in odd, general terms that love was not all it was cracked up to be. There was no talk of work, only of the depression she was going through. One sentence was clearly fixed in Annabel's mind still: 'Piers says he will never marry me'.

Annabel had cursed Piers Bellingham for playing around with her friend's feelings, and had resolved to write a long, comforting letter in reply . . . when she had time. If only she had known how bitterly she was to regret not getting in touch with Kate straight away. If she had acted at once, it might . . . just might . . . have made a difference.

Christmas had seemed no less hectic than the end of term. Family and friends' parties whirled her through the holiday, and she arrived back for the spring term with the promised letter still not written and destined never to be so.

Kate was dead. College rang with one horrified version after another. An accident in Holborn underground station before Christmas . . . a verdict of death by misadventure . . . Wasn't it awful? Shattering? Horrific?

Annabel couldn't forget that one sentence in Kate's letter: 'Piers says he will never marry me'. She felt convinced that her friend's death was no accident, but she could do nothing about it. She had never met Kate's family, and in any case, what would be the point of crashing in on their grief now with the awful suggestion that their daughter's death might have been suicide? Nothing could bring Kate back now, and further probing into the cause of the accident could only deepen her parents' suffering.

From that moment on, the name of Piers Bellingham stood for all that was evil in Annabel's mind. He had taken her friend, worked her until she was out of her mind, so centred her life on him that there seemed nothing in life *but* him, then coldly withdrawn himself. And Kate ... poor, warm, emotional Kate, had been unable to take it.

There was more to it than that, of course. In the shadow of Annabel's hatred was guilt. Guilt that she herself had held back until it was too late. She would carry that burden with her always.

She shivered and realised that the bath water was almost cold and the light beginning to fade outside. Brooding could do nothing. In turning down Piers Bellingham's offer she had taken the only action that meant anything now. In the mean time, no doubt her friends were already waiting for her at Gino's.

Half an hour later Annabel was on her way, trim and slight in a black and white Sheridan Barnett long skirt and top, a miraculous find in an 'As-New' shop sale. Her hair was a glossy dark mass, and only the shadows still lingering in her grey eyes betrayed the thoughts that caused them.

Gino's was within walking distance of the flat, just the other side of St Barnabas Square. Annabel walked off some of her low spirits, and by the time she came to the Square itself she was beginning to feel less likely to put a damper on the evening's party.

St Barnabas Church had gone in some earlier period of reconstruction and the Square was turned into a garden where Annabel had often come to sit and read on sunny afternoons, finding its leafy greenness an oasis in the dusty city.

Francis Moore lived in one of the houses overlooking the Square, and just in time she saw him come out of his brightly lit doorway with a can and go over to peer inside the raised bonnet of his car.

Catching her breath, Annabel slipped across the road and into the garden before he could see her. Having set up this afternoon's abortive meeting, he wouldn't be feeling too sweet towards her now.

She glanced back before disappearing into the concealing shadows of the shrubbery. Good. He was absorbed in what he was doing.

'Mind the dog!'

Just in time she stopped. A little Manchester terrier had shot out of a side path in front of her feet, and its owner's hand caught her arm and steadied her.

'Sorry! My fault,' Annabel began. 'Oh!' The exclamation came when she realised with an unpleasant jolt that the dog was Francis Moore's Mac, and the person on the other end of the lead was Piers Bellingham. He was looking equally surprised to see her, and the light from the street lamp emphasised the fine-drawn, sardonic lines of his face.

'What are you doing here?' Annabel asked awkwardly.

'Hardly expecting to see you again quite so soon. Here, Mac!' He tugged the straining dog sharply, and it sat obediently at his feet. 'As a matter of fact, I've just had a very pleasant meal with Francis and his wife, and once his radiator's topped up he's taking me to the station. However, since Fate has so kindly arranged this meeting, let me urge you again to reconsider what I said this afternoon.'

He was taking another card from his pocket, and Annabel clasped her hands childishly behind her back and stepped away from him in annoyance.

'Please don't re-open that subject. Before I leave for home tomorrow, I shall be calling on Doug Ryman to see what he has lined up for me.'

'That's right.' He deliberately ignored the meaning of

what she had said, picking only on the words that suited him. 'Talk to Doug. He'll make you see sense.'

He reached out and tucked the card into the low neckline of her top, and she felt his fingers warm against her flesh for a second, then the cold edge of the card was scratching her.

'Give me a ring afterwards,' he went on, his eyes amused at her involuntary shrinking away from his touch.

'Can't you take no for an answer?' she burst out angrily, groping for the card.

'I don't believe I can. And I've told you, I'm determined to have you ... on my books, that is.' The pause was deliberate, and offensive. It was probably the way he would have spoken to anyone who crossed him in his intentions, but the words seemed intensely personal ... threatening even.

Annabel did not trust herself to speak again. She turned sharply away and walked across the garden away from him. At the intersection of the paths in the centre there was an old-fashioned Victorian street lamp, its pool of light falling on a rubbish bin. She stopped, and slowly, deliberately tore the card into tiny pieces, letting them flutter down to join the ice-cream wrappers and orange peel segments that she could smell lying there.

'And I hope you were watching that, Mr Fancy-Yourself Bellingham!' she said to herself as she walked on into the shadows.

CHAPTER TWO

'YOUR name seems to have been crossed out. I was late in this morning because of a dental appointment. Let me just check with Mr Ryman.'

Doug's middle-aged secretary gave Annabel a friendly smile and disappeared through the door beyond her desk. Annabel looked round at the shabby furniture and the walls that cried out for fresh paint. There were a few brave touches, thanks, no doubt, to the secretary—a thriving pelargonium on a table near the window, and the smell of furniture polish in the air. But who, in a busy office, has time to water the plants and spray the furniture mid-morning? She frowned at her own thoughts. Those three last night had really got to her with their unceasing arguments. She was seeing Doug Ryman's office through their eyes, not her own.

'What's all this, then? I didn't expect to see you at all!' Doug's round face appeared in the doorway, his tie tugged loose and the top button of his shirt either undone or missing.

'Sorry about all the clutter. I'm catching the lunchtime coach home.' Annabel indicated the case and bags at her feet. 'We did say eleven o'clock, didn't we?'

'I thought it had been un-said, but never mind. I'll just cancel Lady Muck and the Right Honourable Joe Bloggs and see if I can squeeze you in.' Grinning, and with exaggerated stagey gestures, Doug shepherded his secretary back to her desk and Annabel through to the office.

'What do you mean "un-said"?' she asked as she took the chair in front of Doug's untidy desk, her eyes drawn, with echoes of last night's argument, to the half-eaten croissant on a paper bag which he was busily bundling up and stuffing into a wire tray marked 'Urgent'. 'Am I going mad, or did we arrange to have a chat before I went home?'

'We did, love. But when Bellingham phoned this morning I just put a line through you. Shouldn't I have done?'

'When *who* phoned?' Annabel leaned forward, her voice dangerously controlled.

'Piers—Piers Bellingham. Letting me know he's offered you the shelter of his mighty wing, so to speak.'

'He had no right!' Annabel jumped up, unable to contain her rage. 'Absolutely no right at all to poke his nose into my affairs, cancelling my appointments, playing God! Who does he think he is?'

'Hang on a minute——' Doug leaned back in his chair, shrewd eyes on her burning face, hands linked across his stomach. 'I didn't say he cancelled your appointment. *He* said he'd offered to take you on. *I* was the one who cancelled.'

'Then you're as bad as he is. If I make an appointment, I keep it. And if anyone does any cancelling, it's going to be me, not Mr Almighty Bellingham!'

Doug registered her turn of phrase with an approving nod. 'Good, that. Suits him. I must remember to try it out on him next time he comes slumming.' He got up and came round the desk, where he took Annabel gently by the arm and led her back to the chair, sitting her down again and patting her head as he would a dog. 'Now look, love. This is a small room to shout in, and my secretary's very sensitive. I know your lungs are well trained and all that, but let's take it gently, shall we?'

'Sorry, Doug, but that man brings out the worst in me. He did suggest himself as my agent last night, but believe me, I told him straight away that there was nothing doing. You were my man, I said, and I don't go back on my word. That's exactly how it went.'

'Then you want your little head examined, don't you?'

Annabel exhaled a long, incredulous breath. She couldn't understand this. She would have expected him to be hurt at the prospect of being gazumped by Piers Bellingham, but his good-natured face showed no signs of any such feelings.

'You can't mean you think I should have jumped at the chance, surely?' she asked.

'What else, doll? He's a good man.'

She stared at him. 'Do you mean *good*, good? Or *clever*, good?'

'Both, for all I know.'

But not in her book. Not in a million years. 'I don't like him,' she said flatly.

'You don't have to. It doesn't get written into the contract.'

'Oh, Doug!' She slumped back in her chair. 'You're getting me all confused. When I walked in here, everything was crystal clear.'

'You *think* it was, you mean. Look, love, let me put it to you straight. I'm a small fish. I'd do my best for you because I know good stuff when I see it. I'd get you the odd concert at the Town Hall, maybe; a *Messiah* or two round Christmas; perhaps even stretch as far as a fancy recital in the National Trust places now and then. But that'd be it, the lot. God knows how you'd live. Now tell me straight: what do you see yourself doing? In your wildest dreams, I mean.'

Annabel was forced into honesty by his own straightforwardness. 'Opera. It's what I've always wanted.'

'And we only get the occasional treat when the Welsh National comes visiting.' Bleak grey eyes and knowing, faded blue ones locked for a moment. 'Now our friend the Almighty,' Doug went on, 'he knows people. He's got both feet in doors. He carries the right sort of visiting card.'

'Doug, you're your own worst enemy,' Annabel said limply.

'Maybe, according to some people's ideas, but I do all right for me. The thing is, could I do all right for you, love? That's the question, and the answer—now that you've got an option—has to be no. I jog along quite happily. I've got enough and I don't want more. But the Almighty, bless him, wants the lot—for his own pride and for those he represents. And that's the sort of agent you should have.'

'But I still don't want to be involved with him!' she cried. 'I trust you.' Doug was the genuine article: an honest man. It was written all over his face. So why don't I take his advice, then? Annabel thought with sudden logic. The sensible thing to do would be to follow his recommendation, acknowledge that it was stupid to let the past affect the future. Could she ever make a career for herself if she thought that way?

Doug got up and came round the desk again to put a hand under her chin and turn up her brooding face.

'Listen—you trust Uncle Doug. This is what you do, love,' he said. 'You take a look at my card index here.' He turned her head and with his free hand pulled open a grey metal filing box. 'This is you: Annabel Foley. Now that card's going into my "pending" tray. "Pending" means things I do nothing about, if you need a translation.' He tossed the card on to a pile of letters and bills. 'So away you go, free as a bird. Have a good think—a *clear* think. Do the right thing for you. And if ever you need to turn up on my doorstep again, that card goes back pronto into the index, and we start afresh from there. Right?'

'I have a feeling it'll be sooner than you think, Doug,' Annabel sighed, her voice troubled and full of doubt.

He wiggled her chin. 'We'll see about that. Remember—the best for *you*. Nothing else.'

So much for rejecting one card and tearing up another. She was going to need that wretched telephone number after all, but no doubt Directory Enquiries would know such an important man's number by heart, though, she thought, her lip curling as she walked to the coach station. She was not in any hurry to eat humble pie. A lot of reflection was going to take place before that.

The journey did nothing magic to clear her thoughts, merely reinforcing the two alternatives already in her mind, neither of them attractive. She could either put herself in Piers Bellingham's hands and loathe it, or not do so and regret it despite herself.

There was a local bus in the coach station when they pulled into the Oxford terminus, so Annabel didn't bother phoning her mother for a lift as they had arranged. It would be nice to surprise her.

Lindhurst, the faintly shabby Victorian house that had been home for as long as she could remember, hadn't changed—and there was the familiar smell of delicious baking as Annabel opened the front door.

'Hi! I'm home!' she called, dumping her baggage on the polished parquet. There was an exclamation from the direction of the kitchen and her mother came hurrying out, flour streaking her still dark hair, her eyes—a calmer version of Annabel's stormy grey ones—lighting up with pleasure.

'Annabel! Why didn't you ring? We were waiting for the phone.' She hugged her daughter, an embrace which Annabel accepted philosophically as the assessment her mother's next words confirmed it to be. 'You're so thin! Come on into the kitchen. I've just finished baking.'

'Fatted calf time already?' Annabel followed her mother into the kitchen and jumped as someone stepped out from behind the door to surprise her. 'Dad! What are you doing home? I didn't see your car.'

'Surprises all round!' His bone-crushing hug had no ulterior purpose. 'So sorry we missed *Figaro*, darling. How did the last night go?'

'Very well, so everyone said. I've brought the *Post* with a crit in it. How's the cold now? It must have been a bad one. I've never known you miss anything I had a part in before.'

Her parents exchanged glances that Annabel couldn't quite interpret.

'Go on, Tom,' her mother said gently. 'We said there'd be no more pretending once Annabel was home. You'd better tell her now, love.'

'What's the matter?' Annabel looked from one face to the other, seeing suddenly that her father looked tired and paler than usual, and that there were tiny new vertical stress lines on her mother's forehead.

Her father gave a little shrug of resignation. 'Well, let's at least have a cup of tea in front of us, then, Mary.'

The cups were already there and the tea made. Annabel got an extra cup for herself while her mother cut slices of warm apple cake.

'Go on, Dad, please!' she urged. 'You've got me worried.'

'No cause for undue worry,' her father told her, taking off his gold-rimmed half-glasses and polishing them: the action—a familiar decoy—contradicting the words. 'The fact is, Annabel, that there never was a cold. Something happened about a week before your production that we thought it was better not to tell you about at that particular point. We know how susceptible that voice of yours can be to your mental and physical state.' He smiled at her and hesitated, then steeled himself to go on. 'The fact is that, like so many other people, I've been made redundant, I'm afraid.'

Although his voice was matter-of-fact, Annabel knew how undermined her father's confidence would be. A gentle, non-competitive man, he had taken until the age of fifty-five to reach management level in the small precision tool-making firm in which he had spent all his working life. To be cast off having once achieved that status would be a bitter blow to him, no matter how he tried to conceal it.

'Oh, Dad! I'm so sorry,' she said, reaching out to put her hand over his. 'That's rotten. How could they?'

'They couldn't help it. The usual take-over story, and what they pleasantly call "rationalisation". I wasn't the only one.'

'But you're so good at your job. When I think how many emergencies you've been called in to see them through . . .

Oh, damn them! I'm sure you'll get another job.'

Her father shook her head. 'Not at my age, love. One must be realistic.'

'But we've got plans, haven't we, Tom?' her mother interjected, her voice positive and cheerful as Annabel remembered it being in many a past crisis. 'That was the main reason for staying put—next to the wish not to upset you. We wanted to get ourselves sorted out and have some prospect in view—and now we have.'

'So what is it? I suppose you'll sell this house at last? If you moved to a flat that would release quite a lot of capital, wouldn't it?'

'We're doing the opposite, actually,' her mother smiled. 'The idea is that we take in students. With two attics and all these bedrooms we can put in an extra kitchen upstairs and still let four or five rooms.'

'The four or five being dependent on whether you'll be around and require your old room on a fairly permanent basis,' her father said. 'And downstairs can be converted into a flat fairly easily. We've had plans drawn up already.'

'Why don't you get them and show Annabel, Tom?' her mother suggested, and he got up eagerly and disappeared in the direction of the study.

'How has he been?' Annabel asked her mother softly.

'Absolutely shattered at first—I'll never forget his face the day they told him. You know how he hates to make a fuss about anything . . . He's still not sleeping too well, but once we'd hit on this idea and there was something else to think about he bucked up very quickly. Sh! Here he comes.'

'The great thing about these old houses,' her father said as he spread papers all over the table, pushing aside plates of uneaten cake, 'is that there are so many rooms to play with when it comes to a scheme like this.' He explained in detail just what changes would have to be made to the house to give them adequate comfort and privacy from their prospective tenants.

'It looks expensive . . .' said Annabel, knowing that surplus cash had never been much in evidence and was likely to be even less so now. 'How will you manage the initial bit? A loan?'

'No. The redundancy money and what we got for my car—which was this year's registration, fortunately—will just about cover it. Once the conversion's done we'll be sure of continued demand for rooms. They're always at a premium in Oxford. So we should be all right. Maybe better than before, with my pension.'

'Oh, Dad! You haven't had to get rid of your precious dream car!' The pain she imagined him feeling was reflected in Annabel's face. 'You've only just got it after all those years of talk!'

'It doesn't matter really, poppet. The talk was the best part—it often is. And we certainly don't need two cars around with both of us at home. Your mother's drinks far less petrol, anyway.'

His smile was almost convincing, but Annabel was in no doubt about the disappointment. She watched him roll up the plans, feeling totally inadequate.

'Now that's quite enough about us,' he said. 'What about your plans? Anything in the offing?'

Annabel's intention to talk things over with her parents evaporated instantly. Whatever she had been going to tell them about her hesitation to take up Piers Bellingham's offer could not possibly be said now. There was no way that she could say to a man who had been so recently made redundant: 'Look—I've been given this great opportunity by a London agent, but I don't know whether I fancy taking it up or not.' Nor could she hang around waiting for something else to turn up, being a continuing financial liability on her parents with things as they were.

'Great news!' she said, hoping her voice sounded less false to them than it did in her own ears. She went on to give them an edited account of her encounter with Piers Bellingham, and the effort it cost her was worth while when she saw the delight and relief on her parents' faces.

'I don't mind telling you now,' her mother said with her usual honesty, 'we've been rather worried about what you would do, love. It's not an easy life you've chosen for yourself. If this man is as good as you say he is, you could be saved a lot of heartache.'

On the other hand, I could be letting myself in for a load of trouble, Annabel thought bitterly. But it was done now. The words were said. Now she must follow them up.

'I have to phone the man,' she told her parents, looking at the pine clock on the wall. It was five forty-five. 'I'd better do it now. Maybe he'll still be at the office. I'm sure he's the kind who always works late.'

While she waited for Directory Enquiries to come up with the number Annabel couldn't quite suppress the hope that no one would answer and she would have a reprieve until morning, at least. But the bell only rang once before a clipped voice spoke.

'Bellingham.'

She felt an irritating tremor of schoolgirl nervousness.

'This is Annabel Foley,' she began.

'Is it, indeed? You certainly took your time. You saw Doug at eleven this morning, I understand.'

Her fingers tightened round the receiver. His tone and the implication that he knew her answer already annoyed her instantly, but her parents were only in the next room. She couldn't say anything that would disturb them.

'I was very surprised to learn that you had contacted Mr Ryman,' she said. And that was a blue-pencilled version of what she had really felt if ever there was one.

'Were you? Would you have told him of my offer?'

'No, I wouldn't.'

'Exactly. So there you have my reason for speaking to Doug. Incidentally, he's an old business contact of mine, and there'll be no hard feelings no matter what transpires between you and me. I take it that you've come to a decision?'

'I have.' Annabel steeled herself for the words. 'I—I've considered everyone's advice, especially that of Mr Ryman, and I've decided to talk over your offer with you. I don't know exactly what you have in mind for me—and I have very strong ideas about what I want to do.'

'Of course. And I agree that we need to meet and get down to some sensible discussion,' he said smoothly. 'In the mean time I am very glad that you've come to the right decision.'

Smug, patronising bighead! Annabel thought savagely.

'Are you speaking from the Midlands?' he went on.

'No, I'm at home. At my parents' home.'

'And that's where?'

'Oxford.'

'Really? In that case . . . let me see . . .' There was the dry sound of pages being turned over quickly. 'I'm fairly well booked up this weekend, and next week's busy too as far I can see . . . Yes. It might as well be tonight. It's now six o'clock. I could be with you in an hour. That's all right, I presume?'

It was more of a statement that a question, and Annabel didn't like the way pressure was building up on her.

'You can't want to rush off straight from the office,' she hedged. 'What about your meal?'

He gave a short laugh. 'If I let regular mealtimes worry me, I should do nothing!'

She kicked the door of the study shut and spoke urgently. 'Look, I don't know that it would be a good idea at all. Things are difficult here. I've just heard that my father has been made redundant.'

'I'm sorry—but don't you think it will ease at least some of his worries to hear at first hand that he has no need to be troubled on your behalf?'

'I don't know about that . . .'

'Then take my word for it. And your parents will naturally want to meet me and talk things over.'

'I'm not a child!' she said sharply. 'I make my own decisions, Mr Bellingham.'

'No one who saw your Countess would be under any misapprehension that there was much of the child about you,' he said, his voice amused. 'I'm merely saying that your family will want to be reassured that their daughter—entirely as a result of her own decision, of course—is in safe and competent hands.'

Safe hands . . . Annabel thought of Kate with a shudder.

'Have you planned to go out this evening?' he pressed impatiently.

'No. I've only just arrived home.'

'Then I shall be with you no later than seven-thirty for an hour of your time—no more. Give me your address.'

When she put the phone down, Annabel felt as though she had been skilfully managed into agreeing with everything Piers Bellingham wanted her to do. No doubt that was the way he was used to doing things. Well, he had a surprise coming to him. She wasn't going to be pushed around and manipulated by any man, and by him in particular. He had a lot to answer for, and he would find things wouldn't go as smoothly with her as with his countless other women.

'I'm afraid he insisted on coming over right away,' she told her parents. 'He'll be here in about an hour.'

Their reaction annoyed her.

'That's good of him,' her father remarked. 'Not much fun rushing across country at the end of a working day.'

'The poor man must eat with us,' her mother said. 'The casserole's plenty big enough for four, so all I need do is prepare a few more vegetables. There's a fresh apple pie and cream . . . and I've got a melon that should be just right in the larder.' She was bustling round the kitchen as she spoke, tidying away the tea things. 'I think the dining-room since it's a rather special occasion, don't you? And have we a bottle of red in the cellar, Tom? It's beef.'

'For heaven's sake!' Annabel said sharply. 'The man's an agent, not a member of the Royal Family. He's going to make money out of me. We don't have to roll out the red carpet.'

'Have we ever not welcomed your friends?' her mother said in gentle reproof.

'He's not my friend. Definitely not. He's business. Oh——' She broke off, hating the petulant sound of her own voice. 'I'm going to take my things upstairs.' She went

out of the kitchen, feeling like the child she had denied
herself to be.

Any thought Annabel had that her parents would
understand her reaction once they met Piers Bellingham
was quickly killed.

He had given a perceptive, glinting smile at her cursory
greeting, quite aware, she was sure, that she had
deliberately made no attempt to dress as though this
evening was special. Then he had set out to charm her
mother and father. She had watched his polished operation
all through dinner. He was wearing grey slacks and a paler
grey sweater—casual dress for which he apologised,
managing to tie the apology in with a compliment on her
mother's appearance and her 'charming table'. Annabel
was ready to lay any bet that the sweater was kept in a file
marked 'Clients' families: reassurance of.' No doubt he had
a dependable tweed jacket in the car to complete the
illusion. But she remembered the dark, threatening figure
of the night before, and she was not taken in one jot.

The conversation had run on smoothly, somehow
managing to exclude Annabel. He would have to address
her directly soon when he moved from generalities and got
down to business, she thought angrily.

When coffee was poured he indicated that they must now
talk seriously and charmingly brushed aside her parents'
offer to leave them in private.

'You must both be eager to know what Annabel will be
doing,' he said with a smile. Annoyed at still being the
outsider, talked about rather than with, Annabel put her
cup down on the table with a rattle which earned her a

hooded glance of amusement before he turned back to her parents.

'The first priority will have to be some intensive voice coaching,' he began.

'There are no funds for expensive lessons,' Annabel said firmly.

He smiled patiently. 'If you hear me out, Annabel, all that will be explained.' Not a bit put out by her expression, he turned back to include her parents again. 'Marta Kane has coached several of my clients—you may have heard of her?'

'Marta Kane!' Annabel, having resolved to sit back and say nothing, couldn't suppress an exclamation at the mention of the famous soprano's name. She was retired now, her master classes had been featured on television, and to be coached by such a singer was beyond her wildest dreams.

Piers Bellingham looked at her with tolerant amusement. 'Yes, Marta Kane. She has a house in Richmond, and for as long as it takes she is willing to give you a morning class.'

'But——'

This time he spoke through her, silencing her with a gesture. 'Part of Miss Kane's house has been sectioned off to make a small, independent flat. This is put at the disposition of her current pupil. Annabel would have the use of it for as long as Miss Kane thinks necessary.'

'I'm sorry to come back to the question of money again,' Mrs Foley said apologetically after exchanging worried looks with her husband, 'but we really have extended ourselves in that direction as far as we can, though I'm sure we're all impressed by what you're saying.'

Piers Bellingham leaned forward and the lamplight

glinted on the smooth black sheen of his hair. 'There's absolutely no need to worry on that score, Mrs Foley,' he said. 'Let me explain. There will be recitals which I shall arrange—small ones leading to bigger things—and for these Annabel will receive a fee.' He nodded pleasantly in Annabel's direction. She maintained an icy silence. Big deal! He was actually acknowledging the fact of her existence, if only on the sidelines of the cosy chat he was having with her family.

'The real source of income for her, however, will be the Charing Trust, which is, to put it briefly, an Arts Foundation based in the Midlands.'

'Why should a Midlands-based trust support me in London?' Annabel interjected in spite of her resolve.

'I was about to elucidate,' he said with exaggerated patience. 'The Trust has decided to set up a Young Opera Group, something on the lines of Glyndebourne but aimed at a less exclusive audience.'

'Opera!' Annabel jerked to the edge of her chair, the blood rushing to her cheeks.

'Yes, opera. Temple Charing House is being adapted at the moment—you probably know of the estate, it's in the North Cotswolds. The building project should be completed by the end of September, and it's hoped to run a mini-season in the new year. My job is to gather together a group of young artists—young, because the Trust's objective is to promote young, promising singers to a youthful audience. As well as the seasons at Temple Charing, quite a lot of touring in the Midlands will be involved. That is the scheme in a nutshell; in the mean time, London obviously offers the best training ground.' His dark eyes looked directly at Annabel and he addressed her personally at last. 'Your living expenses, accommodation and tuition fees would be paid by the Trust. Your own work would provide extra for any luxuries you may fancy ...' He surveyed the jeans and sweat-shirt she had deliberately not changed out of. 'As long as you're willing to make efforts, there should be no difficulty in getting bookings for you.'

'What a splendid chance for you, Annabel!' her father exclaimed.

'Maybe Mr Bellingham feels that the Trust is fortunate to have the chance of using me,' Annabel said. Her mother gave an involuntary exclamation at the unaccustomed sharpness of her words, then quickly turned it into the offer of more coffee.

Piers Bellingham talked on enthusiastically, as though no little undercurrent had broken the surface. He wanted her tuition by Marta Kane to begin as soon as possible to pack in the maximum of work before rehearsals started at Temple Charing—in November, it was hoped. By the time he rose to leave, it was settled that Annabel would spend only a week at home and travel up to London on the following Sunday.

She felt rather as though she was being swept along on a tidal wave as she walked out to his car with him, having been gently prompted to do so by her mother.

'I have the impression that you feel you've not had quite enough personal attention this evening, Annabel,' he said, in no hurry to open the door of his red Audi Quattro.

Annabel flushed 'I've found out all I wanted to know. Anything else is immaterial.' Damn. That was as good as saying he was right.

'So let me make up for it,' he went on. 'You now have one

hundred per cent of my concentration. I mentioned the need for you to make an effort—and the greatest effort will have to be directed towards improving your personal image.' He let his eyes wander slowly from her tied-back hair, still untamed after last night's soaking, to the pale blue sweat-shirt that had shrunk from innumerable washings. She felt him note the patch on the knee of her jeans, the place where the stitching had begun to give at the side of her zip, and the hole in the toe of her trainers.

'It won't do, will it?' Raised eyebrows and a mocking smile accompanied his words. 'This—and this—and this . . .' His hand skimmed over her hair, pulled at her sweat-shirt, flicked at the defects of her vintage jeans. 'You've got the goods . . . but what on earth happened to the packaging?'

His touch had been rapid—light, and at the same time searing; too quick to stop, too bold to ignore. Annabel's cheeks flamed.

'I thought it was my voice you were interested in, Mr Bellingham.'

'On the contrary . . .' his eyes retraced the path his hand had taken, 'as your public will, I find everything about you fascinating.'

Anger made her imprudent. Her grey eyes stared into his dark ones.

'Did that apply to Kate Elston too?'

His face closed as though shutters had been snapped shut at a window.

'How do you . . . of course, she was at your college, wasn't she?' He got quickly into the car, winding down the window as he did so, his decisive movements implying that the subject was not open to discussion. His face saturnine now instead of the smoothly smiling front he had presented to her parents, he looked out at her.

'The Trust will provide money to smarten you up. I shall look forward to seeing what can be done. Never forget that the glamour of an exotic working milieu must spread into the lives of those involved in it. Lesson number one, Annabel.'

He lifted his hand in a brief, ironic salute, and took off, scattering the gravel of the drive.

She still burned from his touch and scrutiny. I shall never forget, she thought savagely. But what I shall never forget is what you did to Kate. I'll use you to get my career off the ground, Mr Almighty Bellingham, but your act leaves me cold. Kate may have fallen for you, but you can rest assured there'll be no surfeit of emotion for you to complain about with me!

She had the feeling that too little response would annoy him as much as an excess had done. And that was just too bad, she thought as she walked back into the house and the inevitable post-mortem with her parents . . . because that was definitely how it was going to be.

CHAPTER THREE

HE WAS waiting at the ticket barrier as arranged on the appointed Sunday evening, a light Burberry tightly belted, its collar standing up so that his face looked darker than ever against it. Annabel could see from his expression as she walked towards him that he was fully aware of the effort she had made with her appearance this time.

She was wearing her 'good' dress—a fine dove-grey jersey that skimmed her slender figure flatteringly, with a big white sailor collar and tight, wrist-length sleeves. Her hair, always luxuriant, was this time glossily disciplined.

He took her case and stood looking at her. 'There's less of the student and more of the woman about you today, Annabel.'

Her pretty little feminine shrug was only half affected—the dress made her feel that way. 'Maybe the learning process has started,' she said, recalling his warning at their last meeting.

The look in his eyes showed that he had remembered. 'Good. Then shall we go? Miss Kane is expecting us, though she has to go out later this evening. You haven't brought much luggage.'

'Students don't have the money for vast wardrobes, Mr Bellingham. Food comes before clothes—and the food isn't Cordon Bleu, either.'

He smiled down at her, and his lean, intelligent face suddenly warmed into surprising friendliness. 'That's all going to change now. And something else had better change. The Annabel who wore scruffy jeans and sweatshirts could call me "Mr Bellingham" and get away with it. Looking as you do today, you make it sound ridiculous. I shall expect you to call me Piers.'

'Will you?' She looked up at him with a little smile. 'Then I shall have to learn that lesson too . . . Piers.'

And that's us off to a better start than last time, she thought as she walked demurely by his side to the waiting car. She had had plenty of opportunity in the past week to work out that if she intended to get anything out of this time with him, she would have to appear to go along with his wishes. She ought to be able to do it: acting was within her powers. Then, when she had taken all she wanted from him, she would drop him as callously as he had dropped Kate—and hope that the fall was good and hard.

She smiled sweetly as he held the car door open for her, thinking how fortunate it was that he could not read her mind.

The charm he had used on her parents was turned on her as they drove through the quiet Sunday roads. He pointed out places of interest on the way, asked after her family, and listened with what seemed genuine interest to the plans for Lindhurst. Soon they were going through the picturesque streets of Richmond, and slowing down as they turned into the Victorian side roads.

'This is it,' he said as he pulled into the circular drive of a rambling old house, ablaze with the full glory of a Virginia creeper. Pointing to a small door to the left of the garages, he went on, 'Your front door—but for now we take the main entrance.'

As she followed him up the shallow stone steps to the huge, canopied front door, Annabel felt a tingle of excitement mingled with nervousness.

Piers saw it in the darkening of the pupils in her grey eyes as she glanced at him while they waited, and moved closer to her while the sound of the bell faded away beyond the door.

'No need to worry,' he said in a low, matter-of-fact voice. 'She's eager to meet you and perfectly charming.' His hand closed round Annabel's arm just above the elbow, and the touch of his firm, long fingers added another sensation to the ones she was already experiencing.

A grey-haired woman in a navy blue dress that was not quite uniform opened the door and greeted them.

'Good evening, Sylvia, I hope we've not kept Miss Kane waiting,' Piers said as she stepped back for them to enter.

'Not at all, Mr Bellingham. She's in the drawing-room if you'd like to go on up.'

She smiled warmly at Annabel, and as they began to climb the oak staircase Piers explained, 'She was Marta Kane's dresser. Now she's her housekeeper and companion, and what either of them would do without the other I can't imagine.'

Miss Kane came across the room to greet them as soon as they reached the doorway. 'Piers! I have been so impatient!' Her voice was as flutingly beautiful as Annabel had expected it to be. Marta Kane was no longer young— her hair was silver and fine in its elegant french pleat and her skin pale—but as she greeted them she still exuded the charm that had captivated her audiences. She was wearing a gown of royal blue pleated chiffon that flowed to the ground from a simple yoke, and the eyes that looked so eagerly at Annabel were of a paler but equally clear blue.

Piers kissed her on both cheeks. 'And now the waiting is over.' He drew Annabel forward. 'Annabel Foley—as impatient for this meeting as you are, I imagine, Marta.'

The singer took Annabel's hands in hers. 'He chose you for your looks, I swear! Do you promise me that your singing is as lovely as you?'

Annabel had never been called lovely before. She had been told she looked great . . . she'd had her quota of wolf whistles of appreciation directed at her . . . but now with two pairs of assessing eyes looking at her she flushed with sudden awkwardness.

'I only hope I sing well enough to be a rewarding pupil, Miss Kane,' she said. 'It's such a privilege to be coached by you.'

'And she's modest, too!' Miss Kane exchanged smiles with Piers. 'Piers, do get us all a glass of sherry, will you? Come with me, Annabel. I insist on being humoured.'

She took Annabel over to the grand piano in the corner of the huge drawing-room.

'Do you know this?' There was a book of songs on the piano, open at Schubert's 'Rose among the heather'.

Annabel smiled. 'Yes, very well. It's one of my father's favourites.'

'Good.' Miss Kane sat down on the long piano stool. 'Then singing it will be no effort. I'm dying to hear your voice, and patience doesn't grow with years, so let's *enjoy* it together.' She played the introduction, looking up at Annabel with such pleasant warmth that it was impossible to hold back or feel nervous.

The song was about a young man captivated by the beauty of an opening rose and determined to pick it for himself. The rose, defiant, swore that he too should be wounded in the process.

She knew the words by heart, and Annabel let her eyes wander round the charming room as she sang until she saw Piers standing over by the drinks table, pausing with that special stillness of his to listen to her.

Suddenly the song took on an uncanny personal meaning. He was the male, intent on making her suit his purpose. She was the rose—the female—secretly planning to hurt him. The words of the final verse held a threatening poignancy that came through in her voice: 'But her days alas were told, Wounded both together . . .'

As Piers' eyes met hers, Annabel felt a disturbing presentiment. Would her time with this man leave her, like the rose, mortally wounded? She dismissed the idea quickly as Marta Kane played the closing chords and looked up at her, her face glowing.

'Yes! Oh, yes!' she said simply. 'We shall work beautifully together. Thank you for satisfying an impatient old woman. It was quite unforgivable of me to rush you over to the piano like that. Now let's have the sherry Piers is patiently waiting to give us.'

The talk was inevitably of music. They discussed the works Annabel already knew and those it was desirable that she should grow familiar with, and it was arranged that she should come round to the main house at ten each morning for her lesson.

There seemed to be more than a business relationship between Piers and Miss Kane. Genuine friendship was evident in the way they spoke and looked at each other. Eventually Miss Kane glanced at the gilt clock on the fireplace and put her empty glass down.

'My dears, much though I would like to go on talking, I must stop.' She took a key from the table by her side. 'Piers, may I ask you to show Annabel the garden flat, since Sylvia and I must leave almost immediately. The place is yours, Annabel, for as long as you are working with me. Sylvia has seen that there is a small supply of food—just the necessities—to help you over the first few days when I expect you will be very busy. I do hope you will be comfortable and happy here.'

Outside, as Piers took her case from the car, Annabel said, 'You were right, she's absolutely charming.' She offered to take the case. 'Thank you for meeting me, and for bringing me out here.'

'I still have to show you the flat,' he said, ignoring her outstretched hand and making for the small door on which Annabel now saw 'Garden Flat' in brass letters. 'Watch your step—this staircase is rather dark.' He took her arm as they walked up to the second door at the top leading into the flat itself, and though his grip relaxed once the stairs were negotiated, his hand remained loosely slipped through her arm as they began a tour of the flat, a strangely disturbing physical contact that she couldn't break without paradoxically emphasising it.

The bedroom with its delicate pink carpet and white and gold fitted units made Annabel exclaim with delight.

'This is lovely! You should see the room two of us shared in our last year as students. Primitive was the word for it!'

'Not my scene, by the sound of it.' His dark eyes were looking down at her. 'This is more the thing ... privacy ... space ... What will you do with it all?' His voice was silky with suggestion, his hand warm and heavy on her arm, his body suddenly too close. The flat seemed hushed, waiting for something else to happen.

Annabel eased herself away, her heart quickening. 'I must see the rest of the place.' Her voice was artificially bright, betraying her feelings as always. Piers gave her an amused look and followed her through to the sitting-room which ran the whole width of the flat with a compact kitchen area separated from the rest by a pine wall-to-ceiling unit.

'You see why this place is so appropriately named?' He beckoned her to look down on the garden with its shrubs and flower beds and winding velvety green paths. 'Marta does most of it herself with Sylvia's help. The garden was a wilderness when they took this house ten years ago. She's an incredible woman.' His arm was there again, this time resting on Annabel's shoulders as he drew her to the window. With his free hand he was unbuckling the belt of his coat and unfastening the buttons.

He must have felt her tense with alarm, because his fingers tightened on her shoulder, giving her a little shake. 'What's the matter? Why do you keep acting as though the Victorian worst is about to happen?'

Annabel felt suddenly very foolish. He was smiling down at her and his hand moved up to pull her head against his shoulder briefly, teasingly. 'How on earth shall we work together if you can't relax? There has to be a bit of light relief sometimes, surely?' He tossed his coat on the settee and pulled out a chair at the table for her. 'All I want to do is talk business. Nothing more sinister, I assure you.' He was busy with papers, not looking at her, and she was thankful for the chance to compose herself.

'First, money,' he said. 'This is a cheque for your first month's living allowance, plus a certain amount in ready cash since I thought it would save you any problem of getting to a bank, although all the main ones have branches quite near.' He pushed a bulky envelope and cheque across the table, making Annabel suddenly embarrassed to accept unearned money from him.

Piers guessed at her thoughts. 'The name on the cheque is "Charing Trust", not mine,' he said. 'From the end of this month the money will be paid directly into your account—this form is to arrange that—and the Trust will deal directly with Miss Kane's fee, so after tomorrow the subject of money which offends you so much, evidently, will hardly come between us at all.'

He was teasing her, but she wasn't going to rise to the bait.

'After tomorrow?' she queried.

'Tomorrow, when Miss Kane has finished with you, we have an appointment with Ariana Blair.'

Annabel's eyes widened at the mention of the designer's name. She had heard of her—who hadn't?

'And,' Piers went on, 'there, I'm afraid, that maidenly modesty will be under attack again, because I've got to supervise the purchase of a suitable wardrobe for Temple Charing's new young soprano.'

'But that's ridiculous!' she protested hotly. 'I buy my own clothes, for goodness' sake. I have done since my early teens. I couldn't possibly let anyone else choose them for me.'

'In this case you're just going to have to compromise.' He rocked back on his chair, staring at her with amusement tempered with determination. 'Think what could happen if I let you loose with a dress allowance. You might buy T-shirts and dungarees and totally unsuitable footwear. As a representative of the Trust, you have to present the image the Trust wants, and I'm here to see you do just that. So, sorry—but you'll enjoy it, really!'

'I shall find it humiliating—and I'm surprised that hanging round changing-rooms is your scene, too. It sounds more like a job for husbands or lovers!' Annabel could have bitten her tongue off when the words were out. She knew he would pounce on them, and he did.

'I could aim for one of those categories if it would make you feel better.'

She struggled with her temper. She mustn't let him needle her into showing what she truly thought of him. Not so soon.

'You must admit,' she said more calmly, 'that for a woman of the eighties to have an escort when it comes to getting clothes is rather out of character.'

'Maybe it's very necessary for a woman of the eighties to be looked after at a couturier's. How many evening dresses have you bought in your short life, for instance? And would you know how to manage that way of buying clothes as opposed to pulling them off a chain-store rail?'

'I suppose not . . .' she conceded. 'But anyway, evening dresses are a thing of the past. They went out with the Ark.'

'It depends what circles you move in. And in any case, we're talking in terms of the concert platform, and of the social life that surrounds opera.' Piers looked at her quizzically as he stood up. 'You have a lot to learn, my innocent Miss Foley. But we shall take it in easy stages.'

He shrugged into his coat and tightened the belt, the shadow of a smile still lingering on his lean features. 'Now I shall leave you to explore your quarters and settle in. I'll pick you up at two tomorrow. And do try to enjoy it. Being looked after can be quite fun.'

He took her hand and raised it to his lips.

'Oh, don't tease!' Annabel said crossly, pulling her fingers away.

His eyes glittered. 'You want me to be more serious?' Before she could suspect his intention he caught her face in his hands and bent to kiss her full on the mouth, slowly, as though relishing the taste of her unprepared lips.

It was a kind of kiss she had never had before, his mouth exploring hers with a leisurely skill far removed from the clumsy embraces of student days. A tiny spark ran through her body from nerve ending to nerve ending in a flare of unwelcome response. She was taken aback by her feelings, until hard in their wake came realisation that this was Piers Bellingham, the man who had so played with Kate's emotions that he had made life intolerable for her.

Annabel brought up her hands and pushed against his chest, feeling even as she did so a second wave of excitement at the warmth and strength of the body she was touching, then almost simultaneously despising herself for it.

'No!' was all she could manage to say, so great was the tumult inside her.

'Why not, when it's so pleasurable?' he said, his voice low and amused as he looked down at her.

'If you think that sort of thing is on the books, you're wrong.' She was gaining assurance now that the physical contact was broken. 'I'm here to work and be instructed in music—that alone. And in case there's any doubt about it, let me tell you that I'll get wherever I'm going through my own efforts, not thanks to whatever kind of short cut you or any other man thinks of offering!'

'Can this shunner of the flesh be my bold eighties woman speaking?' he mocked gently.

'Not all eighties women are potential tarts!' she snapped, stung by his pointed use of her own words.

He laughed then, a genuine laugh. 'You make me feel quite reassured, Annabel. This evening you've been so angelic it wasn't true. I began to think I'd imagined the hurt and angry Countess . . . and the girl who glowered at me all through her mother's lovely meal. Now I know it really was you.'

'I meant what I said,' she emphasised angrily. 'No messing about.'

'So elegantly put! And so difficult to comply with when you look at me like that. I can't promise never to be tempted.' The dark eyes explored her flushed face and lips. 'You know, I had a feeling—just a fleeting impression—that we were of one mind about that little experience until you put me right.'

'You took me completely by surprise.'

'Was that it? And I thought contemporary woman was ready for anything!'

Annabel's lips tightened. 'I think you'd better go, please. This has all become quite stupid.' She went over to the door and held it open. The finger he trailed across her lips as he passed made her twist her head away and he laughed again.

'I'm going to enjoy working with you. Don't ever calm down too much, will you? Sweet dreams.'

Annabel went on feeling restlessly charged long after he left. It was both ridiculous and maddening. She'd had brief involvements with men before—at least, she had thought of them as men at the time, but that was before she met Piers Bellingham. He made them all seem the immature boys they were, and underlined the reason why she had never been even vaguely tempted to get into a serious relationship, though her contemporaries seemed to be falling over themselves to do just that. Of all the people who had kissed her, no one had made her feel shaken like this. It was bitterly ironic that the man to do so should be the very last man on earth she wanted to be kissed by.

She tried to remember the address on Kate's letter, wondering if it was in this very flat that he had begun his relationship with her, but it was too far back. In any case, what was the point of creating phobias for herself about such a nice place? She wasn't going to follow in Kate's footsteps. She was going to use her head, not lose her heart. The loser this time would be Piers Bellingham.

She unpacked quickly, then went down to wander round the garden. There was a seat under a rose arch, and for a while she sat there in the heavily scented air, but when she eventually went back upstairs and got ready for bed, her mind and her body were still recalling what she would rather forget.

Two hours of exhilarating work with Marta Kane the following morning sped by, leaving Annabel both uplifted and exhausted. As she made herself a lunchtime sandwich she thought how nearly she had turned down this

wonderful opportunity. Miss Kane—Marta, as she wanted
to be called—had every quality one could wish for in a
tutor, and she was so thoroughly nice with it. Such a
privilege was worth putting up with Piers Bellingham.

All the same, the thought of the afternoon did loom
rather. Annabel went through her yoga routine before
eating, thinking that a touch of Oriental calm might help.

It had to be the grey dress again; she had nothing else
that she could possibly wear to face a session with Ariana
Blair. Thank heaven it had recently been her twenty-first
birthday. At least when she took off her grey, her precious
one and only set of Janet Reger underwear would do her
proud.

The bell rang to announce Piers' arrival, dead on two
o'clock, his promptness coming as no surprise. He was the
sort who would never be late unless intentionally.

Annabel steeled herself not to remember last night . . . to
smile and greet him as though nothing had happened, and
she was relieved when he behaved likewise.

'How did it go this morning?' he asked as he got back into
the driving seat.

'Very well. Largely exploratory so that Marta could see
what I could do. By the end of the two hours I felt she must
have got a pretty good idea!'

'She's the sort who peels the onion down to its last layer,'
he said with a sympathetic glance.

'But it's the onion who cries, not her! No, I don't mean
that. It was terrific.'

'Good. And I hope you'll feel the same about this
afternoon. We're looking for four items. Two evening
dresses—one quite simple for church recitals, and one a
little more showy for the concert platform. Then you'll
need a couple of things that can do you justice for the early
day and evening social occasions.'

Annabel shifted restlessly in her seat. 'That sounds a lot.'
She had never had more than one new dress at once in her
life.

'You don't have to think of the cost. I told you, that's the
Trust's business. What we have to do is come to some
amicable arrangement on what suits and is suitable.'

There wouldn't be much amicable agreement, Annabel
thought mutinously. He would have his definite ideas, and
it was only to be hoped that she would be able to fall in with
them. She looked surreptitiously at what he was wearing.
At least his taste in clothes for himself was good. Today he
was wearing a suit of charcoal grey with a paler grey silk tie
against a white shirt. Self-confident, understated elegance.

'Don't be nervous,' he told her as they went towards the
mock Palladian splendour of the salon entrance. 'We're
getting the tools of the trade for you, and it's a necessary
investment.'

He was well known. Ariana Blair greeted him personally, her eyes seeming capable of assessing Annabel's size to
within a millimetre while she talked in her attractive
broken English. She referred to 'other times', so this was no
special treatment. Maybe Kate too had sat on a little gilt
and velvet chair, watching girls of unbelievable chic show
off a succession of fabulous gowns like these, Annabel
thought with a pang of sadness.

'That one, perhaps? How does it strike you?' Piers leaned
towards her and expressed an opinion for the first time as
they watched a model twist and turn in front of them. The
gown was white, its tight bodice flowing into a voluminous
skirt, a froth of lace edging the wide, low neckline and
catching in the full sleeves at the elbow.

'It's beautiful!' Annabel's slight gasp of admiration had
coincided with his words. She was surprised by his choice.

She would have expected Piers to go for something more sophisticated. But they reached joint approval too of a black full-length gown of wickedly clever cut for the more low-key recitals, and a little cream raw silk suit, its skirt flaring saucily out at the hem, that could be worn with different tops to ring the changes for daytime occasions. The cocktail dress was more difficult, until a twenties style in dark red chiffon with pretty floating sleeves and a handkerchief hemline appeared.

'That's you,' Piers said instantly.

'Do you think so?' Annabel had never worn anything like it before. Nothing like the rest, either, for that matter. 'We'll see when I try them on,' she added doubtfully.

Piers smiled briefly down at her. 'You don't do that. Your own special dresses will be made to fit you exactly.'

She was embarrassed by her mistake. I know *nothing*, she thought as she was led throught the ivory satin curtains for her measurements to be taken.

The fitter worked with professional swiftness, looking up at Annabel from the floor where she was kneeling to check a hem length.

'Your things will be a joy to make. You have perfect proportions. There's no need to disguise anything, and that doesn't happen often, I can assure you.'

'When will they be ready?' Annabel asked, eager to see herself in all this splendour despite her misgivings.

'Mr Bellingham wants them completed within a fortnight.'

'So soon? Can you do it? It seems a very short time?'

The fitter shrugged. 'If Mr Bellingham says something, we do it. He's a very valued customer.'

Again a reminder that Kate had probably gone through this very experience. Kate and others. Her excitement damped down, Annabel slipped on her grey dress again and ran a comb through her hair. Piers was talking to Ariana Blair when they came back into the salon, urbane and at ease in these circumstances as he appeared to be in all. He seemed to have a chameleon knack of adapting himself to his surroundings, and yet he never seemed false. He had been completely at ease in her parents' shabby home. He was equally at ease in this exotic woman's world.

'Not too painful, was it?' he asked as he held the car door open for her.

'You're obviously an old hand. Maybe it gets easier the more frequently you do it.'

He didn't expand on the other times. Instead he glanced at the car clock. 'We'd better get a move on. There's another appointment at four-thirty.'

'Appointment? What now?' Annabel turned an alarmed face towards him. 'We've done what we set out to do.'

'Not quite. This was an afterthought. It may seem a liberty, but I've booked you in at Michael's.'

Even a country bumpkin like her knew that name. Michael cared for some of the most illustrious heads of hair in the country—but what on earth did this autocrat by her side think he was doing now?

'Yes, I *do* think it's a liberty!' she said hotly. 'What exactly had you in mind? A complete change of colour? Stripes, maybe? Shave half of it off?'

'Hold your horses! I wouldn't allow any change in the colour of that wonderful hair of yours—nor would I allow any but the most discreet alteration in style.'

'Oh, *wouldn't* you? How kind. How very kind to keep such careful control over what's done with my head.' Annabel launched into a full-scale protest as they halted in a build-up of traffic, and Piers sat patiently waiting for her to calm down, completely unruffled.

'Let me explain,' he said when it seemed that she had

exhausted her outrage. 'You have glorious hair, but it's just a little uncontrollable. Right? And it's beginning to take off again now.' He lifted a wandering curl and tucked it back with the rest. Annabel jerked her head away, and he smiled calmly back at her as they started to move.

'Have you ever had it properly cut? Really well done by someone who knows his job?'

'I keep telling you that I'm a student—or was. Students are poor. We cut each other's hair. We——'

His hand left the wheel for a second. 'We've had the hearts and flowers bit. Do me a favour and skip the repetition. You're being offered the opportunity to have your hair styled.'

'I don't want it cut off.'

'Nobody said "cut off". Long hair like yours is an asset on stage. All I want is for you to have it really well shaped so that it does its own thing even better—and a bit less rebelliously.'

His sideways look embarrassed her.

'So now you're paying for the hairdresser as well,' she said ungraciously.

'The Trust: part of the package,' he said patiently. 'Come on, yes or no? Quickly! We're nearly there.'

She dithered on the point of giving in. 'I say what I want?'

'You say what you want, but nothing drastic. The original you, enhanced. That's what we're aiming for.'

She was deposited on Michael's doorstep, and Piers went on to his office, telling her to ring him when she was ready.

Michael raised his eyebrows dramatically at the sight of her, his swift fingers lifting and pulling her hair this way and that, discreetly deploring the lack of skill of 'whoever had looked after Madam's hair up to now'.

Two hours later, the phone call to Piers made, her head

feeling distinctly lighter and strangely poised, Annabel watched for the red Quattro in the stream of traffic.

Michael had taken the weight and bulk out of her hair, leaving it light, face-framing and manageable. Instead of a springy, rebellious mass, there was a silken fall of dark waves, and she had been shown how clever cutting meant that she need no longer carry on a constant battle with her hair but could delight in it.

As the car drew to a halt, Annabel found herself strangely keyed up, eager to see her own pleasure in the transformation reflected in Piers' face.

She was not disappointed. He gave a smile of satisfaction.

'Absolutely beautiful!' he exclaimed, his eyes kindling with admiration.

'All artifice,' she said as she slipped into the seat beside him, irrationally compelled to brush away his comments.

'Michael has merely found you. It's like cutting a diamond. Man doesn't make it—he brings out its beauty.'

He didn't start the car, just sat there looking at her, making her burn under the steady gaze of those dark, disturbing eyes.

'Is something wrong?' she asked at last, wanting to break the tension.

'Not really. I have a slight problem.'

Her grey eyes looked at him. 'Anything I can help with?'

'I think so. I would like to suggest something, and this time it's nothing to do with the Trust. I would like to take you out for a meal instead of back to hide your light in the flat. The thing is, will you come?'

There was something so genuine in the way he spoke. This time there was no trace of joking or forcefulness, just an honest, almost tentative request.

Annabel smiled at him. 'I should love to, as long as it's not too grand.'

The Relais des Amis had bleached beams and brickwork with bursts of greenery, and it was just right: welcoming and pleasant. Annabel hardly noticed what she was eating apart from an initial awareness that it was good and different. Knowing she looked her best gave her such a tremendous 'high' that she could have eaten dry bread and thought it ambrosia. She was aware too of the sidelong glances that Piers attracted, and she couldn't help feeling a certain pride at being seen with him.

Two glasses of wine made her uninhibited.

'I still can't quite believe all that's happening,' she said, taking tiny spoonfuls of a melting raspberry sorbet. 'I mean, why should the Trust be so willing to do all this for someone like me?'

Piers looked across at her, the lamp on the table highlighting the planes of his face.

'Maybe you should look in the mirror, then you'd understand.'

'Oh, rubbish! The people who make up the Trust haven't even seen and heard me. They rely on you—and yet they spend all this money on training and offer me a place in this new company. It's very casual, isn't it?'

A slow smile spread across his lean, dark face.

'Is that what you really think? That's just a touch naïve, Annabel.'

His words stopped her, bringing her a little nearer earth. 'But it *was* like that. Nothing happened until you casually suggested acting as my agent after the college production.'

'*You* knew nothing, yes. That was deliberate policy, but it doesn't mean that there was nothing to know. Have you no idea how many young hopefuls are listened to, watched, assessed? I've been watching you since the end of your first year when Moore tipped me off about you.'

She stared at him. 'You *haven't*?'

'You and half a dozen others.' He listed the times he had heard her sing—big occasions and minor ones, during those years. 'And I've got tapes of your sessions with Moore that he let me have. The Trust Committee heard those, and came to several of the later concerts. But in the end they rely on my choice.'

'All that time you were watching and listening . . .' She felt oddly uncomfortable about it, her transitory self-confidence quickly evaporating. 'Why did nobody tell me?'

'Because nothing was certain—and what's the point of raising hopes before a decision is made?'

Annabel looked at him through narrowed eyes, resenting the power he had exerted over her life. 'And do you ever make a mistake? Choose the wrong person?'

The smile disappeared slowly from his face. 'Once. Only once.' He was quiet for a moment, shut in on his own thoughts until he became aware that she had put down her spoon. 'Would you mind having coffee at home? There are things I have to do, and I'd rather like to get back now.'

'No. Suddenly I'm quite tired, too.' And she was. But it wasn't just that. The shadow of Kate was with them, dulling the lights, stifling the conversation.

'Who was it . . . the one you were wrong about?' she blurted out.

He came round and pulled her chair out as she stood. 'She was a very unwise young lady. You don't have to concern yourself with her.' His tone was cold and dismissive, putting a dead end to that line of discussion.

All the same, Annabel thought as she preceded him across the room, you're wrong, Piers Bellingham. I do have to concern myself with Kate. And whether you like it or not, so do you.

CHAPTER FOUR

HER MORNING sessions with Marta continued to be
challenging, but now music filled the rest of Annabel's day
too. Knowing that she had been chosen and others passed
over, people who would have cared desperately if the
selection process had been open, made her determined to
justify herself.

The opening programme at Temple Charing was to
consist of two operas: *Madam Butterfly*, in which Annabel
was to sing the lead role, and *La Traviata*, and although she
had not yet started to work on them with Marta, Annabel
steeped herself in background. She studied, where possible,
the original stories on which the operas were based. She
went back to each composer's own staging directions and
read descriptions of first performances. She played
recordings of so many different interpretations that Marta,
hearing music continually flowing from the open windows
of the flat in the late summer heat, gently reproached her.

'Don't risk making yourself stale before we even start
real work, Annabel. Remember your director will have his
own ideas—and if you fill your mind with other people's,
you may find it harder to make room for his.'

Annabel listened with outward respect, but the only
concession she made was to turn the volume down and close
the windows.

Piers phoned to apologise for not being able to take her

into the city on the day appointed for the collection of her dresses.

'That's all right,' she told him. 'The first time was the difficult one. I don't expect to be chaperoned around everywhere. I can take the tube.'

'I hardly qualify as a chaperon!' There was amusement in his voice. 'Take a tip, though, and use a taxi. Ariana will have huge boxes for you to bring back, and you wouldn't be popular on London Transport.'

She compromised and went by tube, still hardly able to believe that she could afford taxis, but glad to come home in one, dazzled by the memory of her reflection as she tried on the gowns. However close to stock size you were, off-the-peg clothes were not in the same world as things created especially for you. Sheer magic!

She hung the clothes in a separate cupboard from the rest of her down-to-earth wardrobe. Everything she had looked cheap, shoddy and shapeless now in comparison with Ariana Blair's work.

When she had eaten, Annabel tried them all on again one after the other, picturing herself in the various settings for which they were intended.

She had got as far as the red cocktail dress and was looking at herself in the long mirror, an imaginary glass in one hand, and an equally imaginary cigarette in the other—not that she smoked or had any intention of smoking, her voice was far too precious for that—but the saucy sleekness of the dress seemed to call for such accessories.

'Anybody there?' she heard a voice call. Piers! And halfway up the stairs, by the sound of him.

'Yes. Just a minute.' She shot a panicky glance at her

exotic reflection. There was not time to change back. Damn! One more reason for him to think her naïve.

'All right to come up? The bottom door wasn't closed.' He was nearer now. All she could do was put a brave face on it.

'Come on in,' she said with bravado, opening the door of the flat. 'You're just in time for the end of the fashion show.'

He looked her over slowly. 'We chose well. Very well.' The words were few, but his eyes said things that set her pulses racing.

Annabel tried to will away the beginnings of a blush. 'Go on into the sitting-room, will you, while I take this off.' She darted back into the bedroom and deliberately put on her oldest track suit, mint-green and baggy, and about as far removed in the wrong direction from the red dress as anything could be.

He was sitting on the settee taking a package from his briefcase when she came back, and he grinned at the transformation.

'Cinderella in reverse!'

'Or the swan discovering she's an ugly duckling.'

He shook his head, those disturbing eyes lazily inspecting her.

'Not that, Annabel. Never that.'

She went over behind him out of direct view, closed a window that was open, and opened one that was closed, conscious all the time that he was watching her with amusement over his shoulder.

'I understand that you're already well immersed in your arias,' he said when she finally sat down.

Her defences went up immediately. 'How do you know that? And is it a crime?'

'No crime. Marta will have given you all the necessary warnings—just as she told me that you were working far too hard and needed a gentle push in the direction of a little light relief.'

'Marta's lovely, but I suppose lack of real privacy is the obvious drawback to living in a tutor's house,' she observed shortly. 'I like working hard. I always have done.'

'All the same, you should pay due respect to that body of yours. An opera singer needs fitness to give the right back-up for demanding performances. And fitness doesn't come on tap, it has to be worked at. Are you involved in any sport at all?'

'I do a lot of walking and swimming. But I've hardly had time to get into a proper routine here yet. It's a bit unfair to accuse me of not getting myself organised after only a week.'

Piers dropped his briefcase noisily on the floor at his feet.

'What a prickly individual you are! Nobody is accusing you of anything. As a matter of fact I was going to give you the address of a health club quite near here. They've got a good pool available, and the membership fee's reasonable.'

Annabel subsided guiltily. 'Sorry. Overreacting—which proves Marta right, I suppose. Thanks, I'll be glad of the address.'

'Good.' He nodded approval. 'While you're in a more amenable mood, may I also invite you to a party a week tomorrow at my place? A mixture of work and pleasure, I hasten to add. I'm getting all the Temple Charing recruits together to break the ice. It should help when we move up to the Midlands if you're not complete strangers to each other.'

Annabel felt a surge of excitement. 'Oh, lovely! Then I

shall really believe it's all happening.' She was being naïve again. She damped herself down deliberately. 'But you needn't have come round specially to tell me that. You could have phoned—especially when you must be wanting to get home after a long day.'

'I'm on my way home. My house is just the other side of Richmond Hill, in Nightingale Lane.'

As near as that? So he was almost a neighbour. Was he going to be snooping on her when she least wanted it?

'Not to worry—Marta's the only one who will actually see and hear you!' he said, reading her thoughts. He loosened his tie a little. 'It's been a scorcher in the City. The last day for long, boring business lunches. You don't by any chance fancy a walk in Richmond Park now?'

The idea appealed, but she was not so keen on going with him. He saw her hesitation.

'Oh, come on! It'll be good for you—and I promise totally civilised behaviour. Or, to quote your own golden words, no messing about!'

Annabel had to laugh at that, and with the laughter came capitulation.

'All right. I've been sitting around far too much.' As he got up she pointed to the settee beside him. 'Don't forget your parcel.'

'That's for you. Have a quick peep, but then let's get out of here.'

She pulled off the wrapping paper and exclaimed with delight as she saw soft-backed scores of the two operas. She ran her hands over the smooth paper, feeling its velvety newness, transported into a future when the books would be worn and familiar, the roles truly hers. Then she raised luminous grey eyes to his.

'Oh, thank you! These will mean so much more than borrowed copies.' She raised the books to her face to smell their exciting new print smell, and saw that Piers was watching her with amusement. He ruffled her hair.

'Funny girl! I do believe these excite you more than Ariana's dresses.'

'In a different way. These go deeper. Brandy to Ariana's champagne!'

'Let's go, then, shall we? Got your key? You'd better lock the door this time.'

He called in at Nightingale Lane to change on the way, leaving Annabel in the car and saying he would only be a couple of minutes.

Annabel looked curiously at the house, wondering how old it was. The doorway looked Georgian with its white-columned porch and delicate half-moon fanlight. She wanted to see inside, but she was glad that he had not suggested it now. At the party with other people around she could satisfy herself about the Bellingham background with much more ease.

He was as good as his word and reappeared very quickly, wearing a navy blue track suit, its shoulders flashed with grey and white.

She was startled into the realisation of how good-looking he was. Up to this moment she had responded negatively to him on the whole—he was too self-confident, too mocking, too critical, too domineering. But he gave her a quick smile as he got in the car, and she was aware of the lean attractiveness of his face, and of the brown, dark-haired skin of throat and arm as he adjusted the zip of his track suit top and pushed up the sleeves.

'I thought we'd drive in to the Pembroke Lodge car park

and walk from there,' he said.

'Anything you like. I don't know the place yet.'

She was quite unprepared for the beauty of the Park's open fields and woodlands. The evening sun bathed everything with golden warmth, and across the grass drifted graceful herds of deer, moving like clouds over the open wildness that made the proximity of the heart of London seem impossible.

They left the car and walked briskly along the unmade paths towards the Isabella Plantation. Annabel was glad as they went through its glades and past silent pools that they had the magic of the place to themselves, and that Piers seemed as content as she was to walk along the soft, sunlight-dappled grass in silence.

In the far corner of the Plantation he took her arm, squeezing it gently to indicate that she should stop in the shadow of a tree. She looked quickly at him. His finger warned her to be silent, then pointed to a beech thicket near a group of fenced-off huts ahead of them.

Two fox cubs came sniffing out of the leaves, pouncing on shadows, darting at each other in play, until the scent of humans sent them rustling back into the safety of the undergrowth.

'You arranged that specially, I suppose?' Annabel said when it was safe to speak, her face glowing with pleasure.

'Of course—and there's another treat in store. Shall we speed up a little?'

They ran side by side between the two Pen ponds, Piers adapting his long stride to her shorter one, slowing down to a walk again as they skirted Sidmouth Wood. When they came out to the public road beyond the wood, he took her up a path to the top of a piece of high ground.

'This is King Henry's Mound,' he told her. 'They say he watched from here for the rocket that announced Anne Boleyn's beheading.'

The view over London was spectacular. It was near sunset when the Park would close, and below them the Thames was turning from silver to grey. Suddenly the sun, which had gone behind a low cloud on the horizon, blazed out again in a last burst of fiery beauty. The river became a scarlet ribbon and the rich flush of light transformed the world.

Annabel turned impulsively to Piers. It was a moment to share with someone. He was looking not at the view, but at her.

'Poor Henry . . .' he said reflectively, studying every inch of her face. 'If he'd married someone like you he could have saved himself a lot of trouble. He'd never have wanted to look at the other five.'

The moment trembled between them, ready to spill over towards danger. Annabel had never felt so sharply aware of another person. Although they were in such a public place the world seemed to be shrinking from them, leaving them exposed and vulnerable to each other.

Piers' eyes compelled the answering gaze of her own. 'Promising good behaviour is a big mistake,' he went on, his voice low. 'What I'd like to do more than anything at this moment is——'

'But you did promise.' She stepped back, her breathing quickening as she forced herself away from the spell, then she turned and began to walk back down to the car park. She heard him mutter what could only be an expletive, given the circumstances, then his footsteps caught up with her. They were soon in the car, neither of them inclined towards small talk on the short drive back.

'Thank you, Piers,' she said, avoiding his eyes when she got out of the car. 'I enjoyed the exercise.'

'We must do it again some time.'

She wasn't going to commit herself. 'I shall tell my parents how lovely London can be. I'm going home for the day on Sunday.' She was ready to turn away when his hand dropped on to hers as it rested on the open window of the car.

'Just one more thing, Annabel. It's not certain yet, but there may be a chance for you to do a first concert sooner than I thought. The singer originally booked has to go into hospital and if a bed becomes available she'll take it. So keep September the eighth free, will you? And get Marta to go over the work I've mentioned to her. Nothing difficult. Have a good weekend.'

Then, tantalisingly, when she was open-mouthed, brimming over with questions, he was gone. But at least he'd managed to rid her mind of that dangerous moment on the Mount . . . or nearly, she added honestly to herself as she unlocked the door of the garden flat, still more disturbed than she cared to admit.

Home looked very different when Annabel arrived at Lindhurst on Sunday. The builders had worked fast and furiously, dividing the familiar house into unfamiliar units.

'It's a good job you're only here for the day or you'd have had to sleep in the dining-room, darling,' her mother said.

Annabel was trying to sort out all the changes in her mind. 'Aren't you going to feel a bit cramped now, Mother?'

'Don't you believe it! Big old houses can be very tiring.

I'm glad to have my spit-and-polish area cut down.'

'Ha! You don't fool me. I give you a week from the date the tenants move in, then you'll be baking them bits and pieces and doing their washing, giving yourself twice as much work as you had before.'

The activity had made a big difference to her father, Annabel was glad to see.

'It was just what he needed!' her mother whispered as he spread out colour cards on the table in the sitting-room window.

'And trust you to see that he got it. Good old Mum!' said Annabel, hugging her mother.

So many parts of the house had changed character or function that it was a relief to find the kitchen still its old familiar self.

'Some things are inviolate—and this place is one of them.' Her mother ran an affectionate hand over the surface of the old pine table.

One of the familiar copious lunches emphasised that it was still home in spite of the changes, and during the meal Annabel brought her parents up to date on what she was doing in London.

'And what about Mr Bellingham?' her father asked mischievously. 'Is he proving less provocative than you seemed to find him when he came here?'

'He's all right.' Her reply wasn't exactly gracious, and she went on to soften it a little. 'I don't see very much of him, apart from the times when he's some business or other to discuss.'

Not strictly true, but she didn't want to get down to an inquest on how she felt about Piers, because she didn't really know. She knew how she ought to feel about someone who had destroyed Kate, albeit indirectly. She ought to hate him. But how could you hate someone who showed you baby foxes and understood how you felt about lovely new musical scores? How could you hate someone who liked the same clothes as you did—and parks, and sunsets? Life was so complicated. People who did bad things should be bad all through and make it easy.

There was a phone call for Annabel after lunch— Wendy, bubbling over with excitement because she had got herself into the chorus of a company touring with a revival of *Annie Get Your Gun*.

'I never thought they'd have me!' she said. 'I've managed to lose five pounds, and that by absolutely starving myself since you left, but I'm still hardly sylph-like. It's a jolly vigorous show, though, so maybe the inches will melt away while we tour. Now come on, Annabel. Not a word since you said goodbye! Tell me all.' Her voice had lowered suggestively. 'How is it with Piers? Got him eating out of your hand yet?'

'Oh, for goodness' sake, Wendy! Do you have to judge everybody by your own standards?' snapped Annabel with quite unjustifiable bad temper.

'Ouch! That hurt!' Wendy sounded aggrieved, and no wonder. 'What's wrong with me, anyway? As far as I'm concerned, there's never been anyone but Zak, and never will be. Maybe one day he'll feel the same way. So—sorry I spoke.'

'Oh . . . I didn't mean to be so crabby. It's just that Dad's rather gone on in the same way—and you know how I felt about being taken on by Piers Bellingham in the first place. Anyway, I'm really glad that you all talked me round, or I'd have missed a heck of an opportunity.'

She told Wendy about the Temple Charing Opera Group to an accompaniment of shrieks and gasps, and went on to describe the flat and Marta Kane.

'A *flat*?' Wendy jumped on the word, and the telephone crackled with excitement. 'You mean you've actually got a flat to yourself? How lucky can you get? All right, Annabel Foley, when do we all come for a weekend?'

'I don't really think that's on,' Annabel said doubtfully.

There was a short silence. 'Well, it didn't take you long to grow out of your old friends, did it?' Wendy's voice sounded very cut down, and Annabel immediately felt awful.

'It's not like that, really, Wendy,' she said quickly. 'Only this flat is part of Marta Kane's house, and I'm allowed to live there as a favour. I just don't feel that I can ask loads of people to pack into the place. Besides,' she ended lamely, 'there's only one bedroom.'

'Since when has that put us off? We've had a dozen to a bedroom on umpteen occasions.'

The worst of it was, Annabel thought, after she had put the phone down, that she really did at the bottom of herself feel a bit reluctant to have the old crowd descending on her in a pack just yet. She was in a kind of limbo, floating between two worlds and not sure where she was going to come down. It was only weeks since she had been a carefree, sometimes silly student, ready to drop everything for a party, willing to sleep on anybody's settee—anybody's floor, even. Now she felt herself to have moved irrevocably on. And she was more than a little suspicious that it was getting to know Piers Bellingham that had made her see her old friends in a different light. Not that she wasn't still fond of them—but they all seemed so young, so impressionable, so—unformed.

'You will look after yourself, won't you?' her mother pressed as she left, conscious that Annabel had been much more quiet than usual. 'Don't go working all hours and making yourself ill.'

'You needn't worry.' Annabel proceeded to tick off Brownie points on her fingers. 'Yesterday I joined a health club. Richmond Park is almost on my doorstep for walking—and on Saturday I'm going to a party. So that hardly adds up to a dull life, does it?'

Ironically it was as she travelled back to London that she felt to be going home, which was a strange state of affairs, she told herself, since she'd been there such a short time and it wasn't permanent anyway.

The following week was quiet, which made the prospect of Saturday's party even more attractive.

Marta went through the items for the concert with her— a group of songs by Schubert and two Purcell arias, all of them familiar.

'You'll do!' said Marta at the end of Friday's lesson. 'Now tell me—tomorrow you meet your fellow artists, don't you?'

'Yes. I've only sung with people I know up to now. I hope we get on well.'

'Especially the men, darling! It *is* possible to sing your heart out to someone you can't stand, but if you find him tolerable it helps! You must come and show me your pretty dress before you go, will you?'

Annabel found out the reason for Marta's request when she complied with it before leaving to walk over to

Nightingale Lane on Saturday evening. A beautifully shaped flacon of Oscar de la Renta perfume was waiting for her.

'A must!' Marta said when she handed it to Annabel. 'And just one little item of jewellery which you must also allow me to provide.'

The little velvet box Annabel took protestingly held the most beautiful earrings she had ever seen, little crescents of stones she hoped desperately were not real rubies, though she feared from their fiery flashing that they might well be, from which hung slender, elongated pearl drops.

'Just right for that dress, and I never wear them. Rubies are for when the blood runs hot . . .' said Marta, confirming Annabel's fear.

Later, as she approached the Bellingham house, the high heels of the red shoes she had bought tapping in dainty, unfamiliar rhythm on the paving stones, Annabel put up her hand to her ears for the hundredth time to check that the beautiful things were still in place. Possessions were a bit of a worry.

The front door was standing open, and a babble of voices came from it—far more voices than Annabel had anticipated. She stepped inside and hesitated in the doorway of the room where everyone seemed to be gathered, looking for Piers in the crowd. He was over by the French windows, talking to an animated blonde girl in a white dress that looked simple and innocent until one noticed that it was slit from neck to waist in front, and that its jade sash matched in a far from unplanned way the eyes of its wearer as she laughed up at Piers.

He saw Annabel, and with a word of excuse to the blonde threaded his way across the room to her side. He was wearing cream slacks and a dark brown polo-necked silk shirt—and as always he looked calm and elegant.

Something in the way the blonde's eyes fixed on them in undisguised curiosity made Annabel return Piers' kiss with a sparkling smile as though it was a routine occurrence.

'You look lovely, Miss Foley, ma'am,' he said, his eyes lingering on the soft curves that the red dress so beautifully emphasised. 'And you smell delicious, too.'

'A present from Miss Kane.' She lifted the silky fall of dark hair to reveal the earrings. 'And these, too. I'm utterly overwhelmed.'

'She likes you. Marta had a crowd of admirers in her day—all showering gifts on her. She won't miss these, I assure you.' He scooped up a glass from a nearby table and put it in Annabel's hand. 'Come and meet everyone.'

He put his arm casually round her shoulders as they began the round of introductions. Annabel found herself meeting, as well as the other main singers: minor soloists, stage designer, producer, musical director and wardrobe mistress—all amazingly young and lively, all throwing Piers' smooth self-possession into marked relief.

The blonde was Vivienne Blake, a mezzo-soprano, and she greeted Annabel in a friendly way but managed to hang possessively on to Piers' arm as they moved on to speak to Philip Young, the dark giant of a baritone, and Hugh Palister, whose fair hair flopping over a high forehead made him look the perfect tenor.

'If you've finished your duties as host, Piers darling,' Vivienne said, cleverly detaching Piers from the little group, 'there's something I've been wanting to have a quiet word with you about.' Her dress gave a glimpse of undeniably beautiful breasts as she turned away.

'And that's how it's done!' said Hugh with a humorous twist of his mouth. 'Good old Vivienne!'

'You know her already?' Annabel asked.

'We were both at the Royal College of Music until this summer. You couldn't be there at the same time as Vivienne without at least knowing *of* her, even if you weren't among the ranks of the leading acolytes. She's got a lovely voice, though—and as for her acting—well, you've only to watch her across the room and you get a very fair idea of that!'

His comments, though sharp, were not bitchy, and Annabel thought she would definitely like him. He was obviously popular and was soon whisked away by a flamboyant redhead in a startling purple jumpsuit.

'Tessa Walker, in charge of costumes. Wouldn't you guess from the colour scheme?' Philip Young's deep voice suddenly broke into Annabel's interested scanning of the milling faces and bodies. 'Let me get you another drink.'

He took her elbow and guided her across the room.

'I've been trying to think where I've seen you before,' she said as she took her drink from him. 'Weren't you competing at Cardiff the year before last?'

'Right! Unsuccessfully, worse luck. You weren't there— I'd have remembered, surely?'

'Only as part of the audience. A group of us went down.'

'Where are you from?'

'Nowhere exotic. The Midlands was where I trained, but my home's in Oxford.'

'You could have said the South Sea Islands and I'd have believed you.' He flicked her dark curls with one playful finger. 'Let's go somewhere a bit more peaceful so that we can really talk.'

They wandered out into the garden and found a seat under the window.

'What about you? Scotland?' Annabel guessed, looking up into the rugged, humorous face that augured well for pleasant relationships.

'Manchester—both home and training, but the family's from the Highlands originally. Piers brought me down here two years ago, but it was a false start. I've been a bit of a bad bargain. After Cardiff I developed a nodule on my vocal chords and thought I'd had it. It's been a long process, but I think I'm okay now. I've been out of things for a long time, though.'

Two years ago. While she expressed interest and sympathy Annabel was thinking that he must have come to London at the same time as Kate.

'I don't suppose you came across someone called Kate Elston when you were first here?' she said, her heart beating faster as she glanced over her shoulder through the open window, making sure that Piers was nowhere near.

Philip's brow furrowed. 'The name rings a bell. Hang on—wasn't she the one who went off the rails a bit—got into trouble over something or other?'

'Don't you mean some*one*?' Annabel corrected.

'No, I'm pretty sure it was drugs. Yes, I remember. There was a lot of talk at the time, but then it all died down. Piers came on pretty heavy about it, as I recall. She was involved in that awful London Underground accident, wasn't she? Why are you asking? Did you know her?'

'Her course coincided with mine for my first year.' They went on talking and Annabel hoped she made sense, but her mind was appalled at the casual reference to even further traumas in Kate's life than she had imagined. None

of the rumours going round college in Birmingham had
hinted at drugs. It was a ghastly possibility that didn't bear
thinking about.

Someone called through the window that food was
ready, and they went back indoors, where she was soon
caught up with first one person and then another. All the
time her eyes were drawn to Piers' tall figure, appalled at
the thought of his even more sinister involvement in Kate's
life. Because of course he must have known—known but
not cared. All he was concerned about was to hush the
business up, to protect his own reputation.

Piers says he will never marry me . . . The pathetic, stark little
sentence kept repeating itself in Annabel's mind as she
toyed with minute helpings of food that looked delicious
but tasted like ashes in her mouth. She managed somehow
to avoid Piers, slipping between groups of people whenever
she sensed his eyes on her, and drinking far more wine than
was good for her in an attempt to check the depression that
was slowly engulfing her.

In the end she had to get away. She cut short the account
one of the minor soloists was giving her of his life story, and
slipped out into the garden. A path took her away from the
party noise and through a shrubbery into an unexpectedly
formal Italian garden. There was a seat there, and she sat
down, hoping that in such an orderly garden the chaos in
her mind would sort itself out. Lost in miserable thought,
she didn't know how long it was before Piers' voice
suddenly intruded into her pocket of privacy.

'So this is where you've got to. You've been playing hide
and seek all evening—I've hardly seen you.' He came and
sat beside her, seeming to be unaware that she drew away as

far as the arm rest would allow. 'Is this approved social behaviour in your circle?' he went on. 'Accepting an invitation to a party and then skulking off on your own?'

She looked at him in the light of what she had learned from Philip, and hated him. He seemed hyped up from the atmosphere of the party, and his bantering tone was utterly repellent.

'I didn't think anyone would notice,' she said. 'You, for instance, seemed very occupied with Vivienne and her little problems. Or maybe they were big ones, judging by the amount of discussion of them that was called for.' What she was feeling made her words—which could have been fairly inoffensive given the right tone of voice—sound rude and nasty.

He stretched out his long legs and folded his arms, looking at her with disapproval. 'Perhaps it would be opportune now to point out that bitching about your fellow artists is a highly unproductive exercise as far as I'm concerned.'

'I wasn't bitching, merely making an observation—as you were.'

'And I wasn't born yesterday. I know every shade of feminine pique, I assure you. And that was certainly one of them. Could it be that once again, Miss Annabel Foley, you were suffering from the thought that not enough attention was being paid to you?'

She looked coldly at him. 'Now is that likely? I thought I'd made it quite clear that what I want from you is a working relationship and nothing more.'

'In that case, why are you so aware of the amount of time I spend talking to someone else? It can't possibly matter to a completely disinterested party like yourself whether I regard Vivienne as an extremely attractive, amusing, entertaining companion—which she is—or merely as a highly competent, musically gifted performer—which she also undoubtedly is.'

How can you dislike someone so intensely, Annabel thought fiercely, and yet still be irrationally thrown off balance to hear them describe another woman as 'extremely attractive'? In spite of everything she knew about Piers, and despite all her protestations, there was more than a grain of truth in his allegations. She *did* care how much he was involved with Vivienne, and she despised herself for doing so.

She stood, and at the same time he too rose to his feet.

'I seem to have annoyed you. I'm sorry for my transgressions,' she said with blatant insincerity. 'And now perhaps I'd better call it a day.'

He looked down at her in exasperation. 'Why are you such a cold fish, Annabel? You could have so much to give ... but you will keep erecting a wall of ice between us.'

She flushed. 'Maybe what you call "warmth" seems to me to be an easy kind of insincerity. Surface fire over true cold. It could be that true coldness that I recognise and respond to in you.'

His face was suddenly suffused with angry colour, and before Annabel knew what was happening he had pulled her into his arms. She shut her eyes, unable to bear the closeness of his dark, burning gaze just before his lips crushed hers.

'Coldness, Annabel?' he murmured, lifting his mouth from hers for a second before once again silencing her frantic gasp for breath with another kiss.

The feel of him should have been repulsive, but against

her will she felt her blood leap in answer to his demand.
What should have been stiff resistance turned to molten fire
as her body found its strange, unwanted, exciting place
close to his.

'So I'm cold, am I?' he breathed against her lips. 'And
you meet coldness with coldness?' His hands slid slowly
down her back to mould and rest on the soft, rounded curve
of her hips while she shivered at his touch. 'I think not,
Annabel Foley. I think not.'

He put her away from him then, and looked steadily at
her flushed face and burning lips.

'Remember that . . .' he said, his voice low and intense.
Then his mood changed and he made a mocking little
gesture towards the path. 'And now I'll take you home.'

For a wild moment Annabel wasn't sure if she could
move or speak, or even if she had any idea where exactly
she was. Then she remembered the party, and the thought
of anyone seeing her like this was unbearable. She felt that
the flare of terrifying feeling she had experienced must
have seared its mark on her for all to recognise.

'I don't want to see anyone,' she said stiffly. 'I'll go out the
side way.' She was humiliated by the unleashing of feelings
she had never had before. It was against all moral codes to
behave as she had done with this man—and it was certainly
against the saner promptings of her own mind which were
only now beginning to surface again.

'People were leaving when I came to look for you,' he
said. 'They'll all be gone now.'

'I want to walk.' She was desperate with the need to get
away.

'It's getting dark. I wouldn't dream of letting you.' His
uncompromising firmness made her pathetic resistance

useless. She walked beside him up the garden in silence, and when they reached the road she let him help her into the Audi. They roared off through the streets, but not in the right direction.

'You said you'd take me home.' She could feel a nerve jumping in her throat, and she was only too aware that she had not escaped—he had let her go. If he decided not to do so, she was lost.

'I know what I'm doing.' He drove on in silence, and Annabel sat gripping the edge of the seat, too afraid to question him further. Just beyond Chiswick Green he stopped outside a church.

'This is where you'll be singing next Saturday,' he said, and she realised with amazement blended with relief that he was once again the professional agent, his mind on nothing but work. 'Elizabeth goes into hospital on Monday, so the recital's on. I heard from her earlier this evening.'

The tension inside her began to dissolve as she stared at the place of her first London recital. If he could speak as though nothing had happened, then so could she.

'I suppose she's very disappointed?'

He shrugged. 'That's life, isn't it? The important thing is for the booking to be filled. Incidentally, it might be a good thing to do something about your name.'

She was puzzled. 'What do you mean?'

'Shorten it. Anna Foley's about right.'

'Are you *serious*?' The fight she should have put up earlier crystallised now in defence of her identity. 'So my appearance wasn't enough? You now think you have the right to change who I am as well?'

'Look at the poster,' he said, unmoved. '"John Grey" is twice as big and readable as "Elizabeth Waterman".

"Anna Foley" would have only one more letter.'

Cold business sense, as cold and devoid of feeling as his discussion of what Vivienne might or might not be to him, as his discarding of Kate.

'Well? Am I not right?' He glanced at her, sure of her agreement.

'You may well be.' Her chin tilted obstinately. 'But I'm not doing it. I'll succeed as *me*, not as some unrecognisable, commercially satisfactory publicity package.'

'I rather thought that would be the case,' he said sarcastically. 'They call it pig-headed perversity.' Then he started up the engine and took her straight home.

CHAPTER FIVE

TOO MANY Pimms . . . that was why Annabel had reacted as she did in the garden. A mere chemical effect on the bloodstream. As for Piers, it had been a moment's diversion, his tongue influenced by the same lubricant. He was amused by her toffee-nosed attitude to Vivienne, just as he was entertained by Vivienne's flaunting of her assets.

He had made the switch to talk of business with no effort at all, and he had made no attempt to touch her again. One jokey demonstration of his super-charm, and that was it. She must be very susceptible indeed if two or three drinks could make a man of Piers Bellingham's character seem attractive.

He phoned mid-week with talk of tickets for a concert at the Barbican on Friday evening.

'Thanks, but I think not,' she told him in the most neutral tone she could manage. 'I shall want to do my hair for Saturday.'

'That's a bit of a clichéd excuse, isn't it? You're not playing the offended maiden, I hope?'

'Don't be ridiculous. What on earth could I be offended about?'

'I think you are. You sound frosty. Come on, thaw a little!'

'Strange though it may seem to you, Piers,' Annabel said firmly, 'I just don't want to go out on Friday night. I want a quiet evening in my own company. Shall I see you on Saturday?'

'Of course.'

'Why "Of course"? You make the bookings, but I know you represent a lot of people. Why should I assume you go around with all of us to every engagement?'

'I thought I made it clear that you were in a special category.' His voice had dropped to a pitch that made the tiny hairs on her spine stand on end.

'Stop that!' she said sharply.

'You *are* offended. Oh, foolish Annabel. I thought you were over that stage by now.'

'What stage, for goodness' sake? I'm hanging up. I shall be ready on Saturday whenever you say.'

'Six forty-five should do it. I shall——'

'Then goodbye,' she said firmly, annoyed at his certainty that he rated so much reaction. He seemed to think she did nothing but sit around waiting for the regal summons to go somewhere with him.

All the same, there did seem to be rather a lot of spare time these days after three years of being perpetually surrounded by busy people of her own age. And spare time seemed to allow more and more thoughts of Kate to creep in, especially after what she had heard on Saturday.

She mustn't brood over the past. What was the good of it? Since work wasn't succeeding in occupying her mind to the exclusion of everything else, she decided to go into town on a shopping spree, and spent Thursday afternoon wandering along the King's Road, reducing her unfamiliar bank balance. The Trust's September cheque had been paid in, and it was strange to be so much in the black. She bought leisure clothes that she could only have hankered after this time last year, feeling delightfully wicked and extravagant.

Exhausted, she collapsed on to the tube, avoiding the rush-hour by a whisker. It was a fairly empty compartment, so when someone sat down very deliberately in the seat next to her, Annabel looked up a touch irritably, only to find herself staring into the broadly smiling face of Philip Young.

'How's this for coincidence?' he said, then raised his eyebrows at all her parcels. 'Did you leave an item or two in the shops, by any chance?'

'The soles of my feet, and not much more,' she said ruefully. 'It was great, though. My first real shopping spree as a wage-earner. How are you, Philip?'

'Fine. Did you enjoy the party on Saturday?'

'It was good to meet everyone,' she answered evasively. 'I'll be glad when we start working together now. The coaching's wonderful, but just a bit lonely.'

'Who are you with?'

'Marta Kane. I have a flat in her house out at Richmond. What about you?'

'Not quite so jammy. I travel into town from Turnham Green every day for my lessons. Look, Annabel, I'm glad I've bumped into you, because after Saturday I got a bit worried. It didn't register at the time, but thinking of your reaction afterwards—you didn't have much idea about your friend and the drugs bit, did you?'

'Not really. And I still find it hard to believe.'

'Then don't make yourself miserable trying to. Not if she was a good friend of yours. I was only half-remembering rumours that flew around. There was never any concrete evidence, and you know how things get exaggerated in the telling.'

She glanced up into his face. He looked concerned, his rugged features serious.

'It's all right, Philip, really. You didn't shock me all that much. I'd had letters from Kate, and I knew she was going through a bad time. I didn't know it was quite so bad, though. I wish I had.' She hesitated a moment, then since the opportunity had been more or less thrust upon her by fate, decided to take advantage of it. 'I rather thought that it was man trouble, actually. You didn't hear anything like that?'

His brow furrowed. 'I didn't see all that much of her. We were all doing our own thing at that time, not like now with a big joint project coming up, and Kate went in for modern stuff rather than classical, so our paths didn't cross all that much. I just met her at Piers' place a couple of times. As little as that—but she was the sort of person you remember.'

'You don't know anyone else who was really close to her?'

He shook his head. 'She didn't seem to get involved with anyone else—not on a personal level. It was just obvious that something was wrong when you compared how she was at the first party with how she seemed at the Christmas one. Piers hated it. When he overheard someone speculating about her, he came down on them like a ton of bricks. Then my throat trouble started and I was in hospital when I heard what happened. It was a rotten business.'

'You can say that again. Poor Kate . . .'

It was obvious to Annabel why Piers had wanted to clamp down on gossip. It wouldn't do for someone like him to be connected with something as unpleasant as a drugs-linked death . . . particularly if suicide were hinted at.

She realised that she had been staring blankly out of the window for some time, and made an effort to move on to less uncomfortable subjects. 'The next station's yours, isn't it? Did you know I'm doing a concert tomorrow at St Michael's? My first!'

He smiled down at her as he rose to move to the door. 'In that case: *in bocca al lupo!*'

'*Crepi il lupo!*'

The odd operatic Good Luck wish went on haunting her

after Philip had got off the train. Thoughts of Piers lingered in her mind, his still, dark presence caught up in the ridiculous words, making them seem sinister. Into the jaws of the wolf . . . May the wolf die . . .

Was that what her subconscious wanted? No. Annabel shied away from the thought in horror. Of course she didn't want him to die . . . just pay somehow for what he had done.

She went on feeling subdued until the phone rang later in the evening, and she lifted the receiver with misgivings, half expecting the sound of that smooth, deep voice of his.

'Hello?' she said, somewhat apprehensively.

'Annabel? Philip here again. I hope you don't mind. I got your number from Miss Kane.'

Relief that it was not Piers made her sound extra welcoming.

'Not a bit. What can I do for you?'

'Well, this is very much a spur-of-the-moment idea. My brother's just phoned unexpectedly to ask if he can doss down at my place tomorrow after meeting up with some friends in town. He's getting here in the afternoon, and he won't be needing his car in the evening. I wondered how you would feel about a quick run down to Brighton with me?'

'*Brighton!*' Annabel repeated the place name as though the resort were at the end of the world.

'It's only fifty-odd miles or so. Wouldn't you like a breath of sea air in your lungs . . . pep them up for Saturday?'

Suddenly the idea of escaping from London, if only for an hour or two, was very attractive.

'Oh, Philip! That really would be lovely. Yes, of course I'd like to come.'

'Good. I'll pick you up around six, then—and if you can hang on for another couple of hours after that we'll have something to eat in Brighton.'

'Great. See you then.' Knowing that the thresholds of her life were not limited to Piers Bellingham and work did wonders for the rest of the evening, and made Annabel realise what a restricted lifestyle she had been forcing on herself.

On Friday evening, wearing the grey and black tapestry-patterned jumpsuit she had splurged so much of her September salary on, she was feeling highly pleased with her appearance and smelling deliciously of Marta's perfume as she waited for Philip. When he was about due, the telephone rang.

'How about a quiet drink somewhere before you embark on that marathon hair-washing session?' asked Piers.

She had been expecting some snag in the arrangements with Philip, and she was completely taken aback.

'Oh—I thought you were in town.' Her heart lurched guiltily. Why on earth had she said that? She was going to have to tell him that she was going out, so it was stupid to fudge around putting it off.

'No. I passed on the tickets to someone who didn't have coiffure problems. So how about it? Just the odd half hour can be spared, surely?'

Annabel took a steadying breath. 'I'm sorry, Piers, but I'm going out after all. Philip Young suggested a run down to the coast, and I couldn't resist it.'

'I see.' He saw too much, obviously, and packed it all into the inflection of the two words.

'It was the thought of the sea more than anything—and fresh air after traffic fumes.' She felt like a schoolgirl explaining truancy.

'Nice to know that something succeeds in amusing you. You don't have to explain. Don't forget you're working next day, though.' His words were harmless. His brisk tone was quite the reverse.

'Of course I won't!'

'Then I won't hold you up any longer.'

The dialling tone buzzed in Annabel's ear. His curt dismissal and the feeling that she had been caught out deflated her for a while, but once Philip arrived and she saw his uncomplicated, good-humoured face she managed quite successfully to put thoughts of Piers and his displeasure out of her mind.

They took the main Brighton road but branched off on to a B-road after Redhill and ran through lovely beechwoods beyond Horley and then for the final stretch through the rolling fields and hills of the South Downs.

They parked on the front and for a time found it hard to tear themselves away from the sea. They walked a good distance, crunching over the shingle, then joining hands and laughing like children as they ran awkwardly back over the shifting surface while the last sliver of sun sank below the horizon.

Later, after a bubbling lasagne at a lively Italian restaurant and a last reluctant pause to hear the soft rush and sigh of the waves, they drove a little way up on to the Downs and stopped at a viewpoint to look back on the town, now twinkling with lights under a purple velvet sky.

Philip sighed with satisfaction. 'That's cleared a few cobwebs away very nicely.'

Annabel tore her eyes away from the silver path the moon was making over the sea. 'Has it been a very hard week?'

'It has indeed. I've had Piers sitting in on my classes. Not to be recommended!'

'I can imagine. He hasn't done that with me, thank goodness.'

'Then he's got no doubts about you.'

She stared at him, her attention now fully held. 'You

don't mean—— But I thought all was well with you now?'

'So did I. Piers obviously doesn't.'

Annabel put a sympathetic hand on his arm. 'I'm so sorry. That can't be easy to cope with.' Her own doubts and fears about working for Piers came rushing indiscreetly to the surface. 'Actually . . .' she began hesitantly, 'I'm not sure that I'll stay with him long.'

Philip gave a slight laugh. 'What makes you think that you'll have a choice in the matter? If he wants you, believe me, it won't be easy to get away—not after all that's been invested in you.' He rubbed his fingers and thumb together suggestively. 'Our Mr Bellingham wants a good return on his money—both for himself and for the people he represents.'

For a moment they were both quiet, Philip wrapped up in his own problems, while Annabel realised uncomfortably that it wouldn't be easy to walk out on someone like Piers.

She kicked at a tuft of grass. 'Let's forget him. He occupies enough of our time. Philip, I feel like dancing. Do you know anywhere back in London?'

'Are you sure? I could have you home by twelve as things are now. Don't you want to be in bed at a reasonably respectable hour?'

'I'm not going to sleep, anyway. I just know.'

He grinned. 'Okay then, I'm game. Let's go!'

So it was after two when he finally parked opposite the flat in Richmond for Annabel to get out. She leaned in through the car window to give him a quick kiss of thanks, and it was only as she straightened up that she realised that she was being watched from the other side of the road. A silent, unmistakable figure was leaning against the chestnut tree beside Marta's drive, and now that she was alerted, Annabel could see Piers' car parked a little way further on.

'Oh no!' she muttered, hardly able to believe that he was here at such an hour in the morning.

'What's going on?' asked Philip, becoming suddenly aware of the motionless spectator at the same time and preparing to get out of the car.

The last thing Annabel wanted was a scene, and particularly one involving someone in as vulnerable a position as Philip was in. 'It's all right,' she told him hurriedly. 'It's only Piers. He must have something urgent to tell me about tomorrow.'

'Why on earth couldn't he leave a note? Want me to wait and see you safely in?'

'No, there's no need,' she said with pseudo-confidence. 'Besides, you certainly don't want to cross swords with him at the moment. Just go.'

'If you're sure,' he said doubtfully. 'I'll be in touch.'

He drove off somewhat reluctantly and Annabel walked across the road, knowing that in the leafy shadows dark, brooding eyes were watching her approach.

'This is a surprise!' she said with an attempt at flippancy.

'I'm sure it is. I'd like a word with you.' There was nothing flippant about the tone of his answer.

'At this time? Well, here I am.' She gave a little shrug, refusing to drop her eyes.

'We'd better go somewhere more suitable, hadn't we?'

'It's not exactly a suitable time for social calls, is it? Perhaps you could say what you want to say here.'

'You can hardly pretend that you're in a hurry to get to bed tonight.' There was a gleam of gold as he looked pointedly at his watch in the light of the street lamp.

'Not at all. Neither can I pretend that I'm pleased to have you watching my comings and goings.' She spoke tartly, thinking that since there was obviously going to be trouble, she might as well speed it on its way.

'I shall be glad to explain once we're indoors.'

He went determinedly to the door of the flat, and short of rousing the whole sleeping neighbourhood, there seemed nothing to be done but trail after him.

He stood watching while she fumbled with the key, then preceded her up the stairs where he switched on the lights and turned to face her as she came up into the flood of brightness. The sight of his face jolted her nastily. He was angry—burningly, frighteningly angry.

'You stink of tobacco smoke,' he said disgustedly, his mouth turning down in distaste.

'Really, Piers! Whatever makes you think you can carry on like this? It's not on!' Annabel retorted with spirit.

'Neither is such irresponsible behaviour on your part,' he snapped back at her. 'Do you realise how badly a night spent in a smoky atmosphere can affect your voice? Where on earth have you been?'

Annabel's stubborn chin lifted. 'Eating and dancing with a friend. And what business is it of yours?'

'No prizes for guessing it was somewhere cheap and nasty—and on the contrary! It's very much my business when you're so uncaring as to spend the night before a first London solo performance getting thoroughly tired and having your bronchial tubes kippered.'

'That's an exaggeration. I'm perfectly all right.'

'That remains to be seen. I've heard far more established singers than you say that it takes them three days to recover from a night such as the smell lingering on your clothes indicates.'

Maybe it was the power of suggestion, but because he had mentioned it, Annabel began to feel roughness in her throat. Surely it was imagination? Both the pub and the discotheque had been thick with smoke, though, but she'd been so pleased to be with Philip that she hadn't given a thought to its effect.

She walked over to the window and drew the curtains, then turned to confront Piers' cold, angry face. 'Now you've given your lecture, is there anything else?'

'There certainly is, or I shouldn't be hanging around here at this time in the morning. I had a phone call late tonight from the man who's organising tomorrow's—no, *today*'s concert.' The correction was made with heavy emphasis. 'James Harding is a friend of his, and he's going to be there. I don't need to remind you of the paper he represents, I see. So your standard of performance—good, bad or indifferent—will most likely go into print. I thought you ought to know as soon as possible. Unfortunately it wasn't soon enough.'

James Harding . . . one of the harshest music critics in the field! Annabel's heart sank. If she wasn't on form he would say so in public in the most cold-blooded, ruthless way possible, if previous reviews she had seen were any guide.

She sat down heavily on the settee. 'Oh God! Why couldn't I have known sooner?'

'If you'd behaved with true professionalism, it wouldn't be necessary to wish you'd known sooner.' Piers stared levelly at her, and he had no intention of saying anything to make her feel better.

'All right!' she flung at him, more angry with herself than with him. 'I've been stupid, but it can't be undone now. The only useful thing you can do is leave me to sort myself out as best I can.'

'You'd better gargle, and do it every hour tomorrow. I suppose you have something appropriate?'

She was eager to show that she could get something right. 'Yes. And a little medicinal lamp. I'll leave that on all night.'

He nodded coldly. 'Do you want to get to St Michael's

any earlier now you know the score?'

She shook her head miserably. 'I'd only get more keyed up hanging around. I—I'm sorry, Piers. I should have had more sense.'

'You should. And so should Philip Young.'

'*Please* don't blame him. He wanted to bring me home earlier.'

His expression did not change. 'See to your throat now and get to bed. I'll lock the door on my way out.'

Without a 'goodnight' he left. Annabel waited until the bottom door clicked shut, then went dispiritedly into the bathroom and opened the medicine chest ready to start work on herself. It had been a lovely evening, but it had all gone sour on her. Piers Bellingham seemed to have a genius for being involved in destruction. So did she, for that matter, she added miserably.

Annabel was taut as a bowstring as she got ready for the concert. The black dress made her look very pale and very slight. She tried her odd pieces of jewellery against it, then rejected them, deciding that not even Marta's earrings looked right against the severe beauty of the dress. She added a touch more blusher and blended peach eyeshadow with her usual grey in an attempt to bring warmth to her wan face. At least she could thank heaven for hair that continued to look good. Her voice she must leave to the kindness of the gods. Today she had been very conscious that she was straining a little for top notes that she had previously soared up to like a bird. Maybe the average kindly concert goer would not be aware of it, but James Harding would know; know and react.

Contrary to her expectations, Piers had no air of censure when he called for her. He talked calmly of anything but the coming concert as they drove the short distance to the

church. In the little vestry where the artists were gathered
he introduced her to the concert organiser and to her fellow
performers—the members of the Percival String Quartet.
The three men and a woman greeted her pleasantly, but
were far more preoccupied with tuning their instruments
and warming up. Piers left briefly to establish that
Annabel's accompanist was already waiting in the body of
the church, and returned only to pass on this information
and give her a brief pressure of his hand on her shoulder
before going to take up his place.

Left alone in the artists' room, Annabel listened to the
sound of the Beethoven Quartet with which the Percivals
were opening the first half of the concert. She didn't feel the
tight knot of nerves now that usually affected her. This time
she had the calmness of dull resignation, knowing that her
best was out of her reach, and the most she could hope for
was a reasonably passable performance.

Piers had certainly surprised her by abandoning his
scolding attitude of the previous night, but she supposed it
was not in his interest to upset her unduly before she sang.
No doubt afterwards she would have to suffer the kind of
in-depth post mortem he had inflicted on her after *Figaro*.

The Quartet ended and the Percivals came back,
exclaiming at the packed church and telling her the
acoustics were excellent. Standing beside the half-open
door, Annabel listened to the brief introduction given by
the concert organiser, and then lifted her head with
unconscious bravery as she walked out to a warm burst of
applause.

Her grey eyes met Piers' dark gaze as her accompanist
played the introduction to her first song, and he gave a
slight nod of encouragement as she began to sing. She had
no idea what James Harding looked like, for which she was
profoundly thankful as she threw all she could into the four

songs by Schubert that were her contribution to the first half of the concert.

The applause was enthusiastic, but Annabel was under no illusion that she had fully earned it. She saw nothing of Piers in the short interval, and she felt no better about the two Purcell arias in the second half.

Piers came through to collect her, and she managed to keep a bright face while he congratulated her and the quartet. She regarded his words as being as much a public performance as the concert had been. What she wanted was to get away, hear the truth and then go home.

Once in the car she found herself unable to prevent slow tears of self-reproach from sliding down her cheeks. Piers seemed calm and relaxed as he drove away from the church and headed for Richmond.

'Why don't you say it?' she burst out as the seconds ticked slowly by. 'You're going to eventually, so for heaven's sake get it over!'

'Say what?' he answered quietly. 'You did the best circumstances would allow, I thought.'

'Circumstances that I created,' she interjected.

'We know that. Why bother to repeat it? You sang well enough for most people to be unaware that the fine edge of perfection we both know you can reach was lacking. And you looked quite beautiful, so I hardly imagine that any of the audience will go home feeling cheated.'

'And James Harding?' she said bitterly.

'For that we shall have to wait and see. There may be no review at all, who knows? A concert at St Michael's is not quite on a level with the Wigmore Hall. Maybe he was having a busman's holiday and not using his critical faculties.'

The tears had been mastered by the time they drew up at the flat, but not the empty feeling of disappointment where there might have been deep satisfaction.

Piers leaned forward to look into her solemn face.

'Would you by any chance like company for a short while?'

'Please,' she whispered. It was what she wanted more than anything.

Up in the flat he went to the kitchen area and made coffee quickly and efficiently while Annabel stood watching him, dazed with tiredness and incapable of action. He brought the cups through to the settee and pulled her gently down to sit beside him.

'Drink your coffee,' he told her, putting the cup in her hands and speaking as though to a child.

She obeyed in silence and after a few moments, fortified by the warm drink, she managed to speak.

'If it's any consolation for tonight, Piers, I shall never make the same mistake again. I'm only just beginning to realise how single-minded one has to be in this business.'

He put their cups down on the table, then, in the most natural way possible, he put an arm round her shoulders and pulled her into the comfortable hollow against his chest.

'The best things always do call for single-minded pursuit,' he said. 'And now you must put tonight behind you. You're not unique in having to learn a lesson the hard way. It happens to us all—and you coped with it rather well. I only hope you'll always ride difficulties as calmly as you have this one.'

Annabel absorbed his comfort with mindless appreciation. She needed this kindness he was offering as a flower needs rain, and his touch was so different that she didn't even begin to compare it with the last time his arms had been round her.

'Next time it will be different,' she said sleepily.

'Of course it will, and next time may be sooner than you think.'

She turned her head to look at him, suddenly wide awake.

'Really? You can't mean you've something on the books for me after this?'

'I do—and especially after this. You must redress your personal balance. And the next time will be in Central London, so it's going to be more of an occasion. Are you ready?' He smiled teasingly at her. 'I've talked the organisers into adding an extra item at the Grand Opera Gala in the Barbican Hall. You will be the "jeune fille" of the platform, featured as such to draw attention to the Temple Charing project.'

'O-o-o-o-h!' Words failed her. That he should trust her so soon made her melt with thankfulness. Piers' face, so close to her own, was softened by such kindness that without pausing to think Annabel put up her hands to his cheeks and gave him an impulsive, grateful kiss.

As her lips touched his the strange chemistry flared into life again, all the more powerful because it was unexpected. The light kiss of thanks changed into a wondering, lingering kiss of discovery ... and instead of moving quickly away Annabel was caught and held by something more powerful than she had believed possible.

For a moment she felt the urgency of his response, then, unexpectedly, he drew gently away. His hands reached up to stop her arms sliding round his neck, and he brought her own hands down, resting them back in her lap with a little pat and standing up in one quick, determined movement.

'I must go ...' he said with obvious reluctance. 'If I stay any longer I'll be tempted to take advantage of a mind that I suspect is suffering from a temporary disturbance. Have a good rest tomorrow.' He ruffled her hair, suddenly smiling at the blush that had caught up with her unthinking action.

'I was grateful!' she said defensively.

'I'm not objecting. Be as grateful as you like in that very delectable way! But tonight I think there's as much vulnerability as gratitude.' He gave her a little salute and disappeared through the hall, then she heard his feet taking the stairs down two steps at a time.

It was a bemused, considerable time later, just before she fell asleep, that Annabel remembered she was supposed to dislike him.

CHAPTER SIX

ANNABEL awoke from a deep sleep to find that it was midday. She shot up in bed, the remorse of the previous night making her feel she should be doing something more worthwhile than sleeping the hours away. But Piers had told her to rest, hadn't he? And the fact that she had slept until now was proof that she needed it, she supposed.

She sank back on the warm pillows, thinking not so much of what had happened last night but of how Piers had reacted to it. What a complex person he was, seeming most of the time so hard, determined and single-minded . . . but underneath there was this unexpected store of kindness, tenderness even, that he had shown when she needed it so badly.

And yet . . . that tenderness had not been shown to Kate, whose need was far greater. The unwanted thought slid into Annabel's mind, bringing guilt that she should feel any degree of warmth for this man who had behaved so callously towards her friend. He couldn't be truly kind, could he? True kindness runs through everything a person does. It isn't selective.

She stirred restlessly. She didn't want to keep remembering Kate, and yet the shadow of the past crept inexorably into the present. All because she had ignored that sad little letter, and now she couldn't shake off the shame that she was profiting from a situation in which Kate had been such a loser.

Oh, do something, for goodness' sake! she urged herself impatiently, throwing back the duvet and getting out of bed. She made herself toast and coffee, and when she had eaten she wandered through to the sitting-room and opened a window, leaning out to look down into the garden.

Marta was out there weeding the borders. She sat back on her heels and looked up at the sound of the window catch.

'Hello there! Come round and have a sherry with me before lunch. I want to hear about that concert of yours.' She had been away with Sylvia for the whole of Saturday.

'I will . . .' Annabel said slowly, 'but you're not going to enjoy the account too much.'

'Like that, was it? It had better be a big sherry, then.' Marta pushed a strand of silver hair back with a grubby gardening glove, looking unflappable. 'See you in a quarter of an hour or so?'

Annabel showered quickly and put on the new white jeans and pink baggy shirt she had bought, tying back her hair with the scarf that matched the shirt, and pulling a face at the sight of her wary reflection in the mirror. She didn't relish confessing her stupidity to Marta, but she had better get it over with.

'Oh dear!' the singer said at the end of the story. 'It's not easy to get into the habit of cosseting the voice, but it has to be done. In the end I got quite good about it. I can't tell you how many people I've alienated by refusing to allow smoking under my roof, or sending them packing if they were stupid enough to come visiting with a cold. You'll learn, my dear. And don't get uptight about last night. It's no bad thing to have a slightly less than successful début. It

leaves something to aim at. Tell me, how did Piers react?
Sadly reproachful . . . or noisily accusing?'

Annabel grinned. 'I had the noisy bit the night before!'
She filled in the details of how Piers had been waiting when
she came home with Philip.

'I fancy that reaction could have been prompted as much
by the sight of you returning with another man from a
night out as by thoughts of the effect on your voice,' Marta
said surprisingly, her face thoughtful.

Annabel stared at her. 'Oh no! He couldn't possibly have
felt like that. The very idea's ludicrous!'

'Is it? I've known Piers a long time, remember. I'm an old
hand at knowing what goes on below that inscrutable
surface. There's something in the way I've caught him
looking at you . . .'

'Well, I'm sure you're reading too much into it this time,'
Annabel told her firmly. 'I'm a business package, nothing
more. Put in the money and get out the voice. Only this
time the voice wasn't good enough.'

Marta smiled. 'Have it your own way, then. Maybe I'm
being too hasty. I'm usually much more discreet. Scrab-
bling about in the garden must have given me earthy
thoughts. Forget what I said, Annabel. I'm a sentimental
old woman who tries to plan rosy futures for the people she
loves. And I do love Piers. I should hate to see him not make
time for marriage—and I know from personal experience
that that can happen.'

Annabel was still rather thrown by it all. 'I don't think
you need worry about him,' she said. 'Having seen him in
action, I imagine he doesn't go short of female companion-
ship—if we're putting it politely.'

'So he has made a pass at you!' crowed Marta, her face

beaming with triumph.

Annabel felt herself blushing against her will. 'I've seen him with other people, don't forget.'

'And that makes you blush?' Marta reached out with an impish chuckle and patted Annabel's hand. 'Don't worry, I'm not going to say another word. You must pay no attention to my ramblings.'

Easier said than done, Annabel thought as she slapped and banged her way around the garden flat, giving it a weekly clean to surpass anything it had had so far in an effort to rid her mind of troublesome thoughts. Piers falling for her, indeed! He wasn't the falling kind. He would string any girl along if it suited him. Not a scheming type like Vivienne, of course, who could prove more trouble than she was worth—but little up-from-the-country girls he thought he could use and throw over . . . like Kate, and like herself, maybe . . . Well, he's met his match in me, she thought determinedly. I'm not going to be one of his easy pushovers. All right, so I did find him attractive for a moment. So what? A mere flesh and blood reaction. But my mind didn't lose control, and that's what counts.

Her charge of energy burned itself out finally in the course of a vigorous afternoon swim and a long walk, and the luxury of several lengthy phone calls to family and friends in the evening brought the day to a more placid close.

Monday was when the report could be in the paper if James Harding had indeed been at the concert in his professional capacity. Annabel didn't want to think about it. The morning session with Marta was a tricky one, and it was easy to lose herself in the problems they had wrestled with for the rest of the day.

When the doorbell rang peremptorily in the late afternoon, however, she knew it would be Piers, and as she opened the door her eyes went at once to the newspaper under his left arm.

'Oh!' she said, her voice falling. 'So there is something. Come on up.'

'Could be worse—much worse,' said Piers as he followed her into the flat. 'In fact, if we're talking of adverse crits, this one's verging on the positive.'

'Just let me read it,' Annabel pleaded apprehensively, taking the paper from him and sitting tensely on the edge of a chair. She wasn't mentioned until the end of the short review. First came genuine praise for the Percival String Quartet with a smooth analysis of their interpretation of the three works they had performed.

Annabel drew a quivering breath as she came to her own name.

'Standing in at short notice because of the illness of Elizabeth Waterman was Annabel Foley, soon to sing leading roles with the newly-formed Temple Charing Young Opera Group. Miss Foley sang a group of songs by Schubert and two Purcell arias. After her closing item, the Lament from *Dido and Aeneas*, I heard a member of the audience murmur that she sang like an angel. For me, an angel still somewhat outside the gates, but this is a voice to look out for when experience polishes the quality which was detectable but not fully exploited.'

'Well?' queried Piers.

'It's a good job he was a friend of the organiser,' was all Annabel would allow herself to say, but the sparkle in her eyes betrayed how relieved she was to be spared public massacre.

'So that's that. And now you'll have to see if you can lure him inside those pearly gates at the Barbican. He'll certainly be there. It's an important event.'

Annabel subsided against the chair-back. 'Well, at least I shan't go looking for trouble on that occasion. Once bitten, twice shy. Will you have a drink, Piers? I've got some lager in the fridge.'

He looked quizzically at her. 'I think we can do better than that for a celebration. I stuck my neck out and booked a table for tonight at Giulietta's. I hope you're not going to object.'

Annabel had stood looking through the latticed windows of the restaurant down by the river on one of her evening wanderings round Richmond. It had bags of atmosphere, but it was definitely the kind of place you had to be taken to. She wanted to go, but should she?

'You've nothing planned?' Piers prompted, his dark eyes resting on her, trying to read her mind.

'Well . . .' she began slowly, seeking some valid reason to refuse, 'I had intended to——'

'Not the hair! You surely can't be meaning to douse your head again? You seem to be turning into a waterbound species of ostrich!'

She laughed, and shared laughter destroyed resistance. 'Oh, all right, then,' she said. 'I'd love to come.'

'Good.' He stood up. 'Wear your glad rags. There's quite a good dance floor at Giulietta's. We must try it out.'

He was looking down at her with a smile that had suddenly seemed to develop something of the speculative. Dancing . . . Annabel thought with a wary tremor of alarm. Touching . . . being held if the music was slow. And why wouldn't it be, in an Italian restaurant at night with the Thames weaving its way past the windows and reflecting the moon?

'I'm not much of a dancer,' she said defensively.

His eyes lazily looked her over. 'I'd say you were born to it. Anyway, tonight will show all. I'll be back for you about eight. You can keep the paper, I've got another copy for the files.'

He went, in that sudden way of his. One day *I'll* be the one to walk away, Annabel thought as she listened to the sound of his departing steps.

She went through to the bathroom and prepared to wash her hair, feeling a flash of irritation that now she was going to think of him every time she did so. Ostrich indeed!

The fun of getting ready soon had her singing away to herself. Her voice was back to normal again, thank goodness. When she was dressed she experimented with a red ribbon round her forehead and liked the effect. It emphasised the twenties look. She did a few trial dance steps in front of the mirror, watching the sway of the skirt, the pull of the material against her body as she moved. It was such a lovely dress. It made her feel like dancing . . . like having fun.

The restaurant was busy, but here too Piers was known and the table reserved for them was one of the best: near a window overlooking the floodlit lawns down to the river, and close to the dance floor.

'Do you ever go anywhere without special treatment?'

Annabel asked when the waiter had left them with the big black leather menus.

'I try not to.' He kept a straight face, but his eyes were laughing. 'Do you want any help with the menu?'

'Thank you, but no. I'm quite familiar with Italian, remember.'

The deceptive simplicity of operatic Italian when you had an English score to refer to for clarification was no preparation for the language of food, she found, though.

'I shall have number nine—*ostriche*—to begin with,' Piers decided, his slim finger running rapidly down the menu.

'You can make that two . . .' At least it couldn't be what it looked like! That particular bird didn't feature in continental cuisine as far as Annabel knew, and the time gained allowed a more careful selection of her main course.

Ostriche turned out to be oysters—the effect of which on the libido is common knowledge. Had Piers tricked her into it? Hardly, she admitted grudgingly, but he probably thought he was in for a good time. The light from the candle lamp cast Mephistophelean shadows on his face, but when he looked up suddenly and caught her watching him, the stern planes softened into a smile far more worrying than anything the oysters might effect.

'All right?' he asked.

'Yes . . . lovely.'

Whatever the reason, Annabel didn't mind a bit that the music was soft and dreamy when they danced after the main course. She gave a contented sigh, relaxing as she felt Piers' arms resting lightly on her hips, holding her close enough for their bodies to move together in easy harmony. His velvet jacket was sensual to her bare arms, and the touch of his face against hers was firm and hard with the slightest hint of roughness to come when she gently rubbed her cheek against his, smelling the spicy fragrance of his skin. He was so dark. His beard would grow very quickly. What would he look like with a beard? Even more satanic and dangerous . . .

What am I *doing*? she wondered suddenly, and he felt the momentary freeze, the slight pulling away, at once. His arm moved up across her back and his hand cupped the nape of her neck, pulling her firmly forward to relax against him again.

'That's better,' he murmured in her ear. And it was.

Annabel banished thought and gave herself up to sensation.

'How much does he mean to you?' The question coming suddenly out of the music-throbbing darkness mystified her at first.

'Who?' she asked bemusedly.

'Philip Young. Your unwise escort on that memorable night before the concert.'

'Oh—him.' Now she understood, and Marta's words raced back into her mind, snatching her out of her trance and making her awkward. 'He's a friend. I like him.'

'And what does liking lead to in your case?'

What he was insinuating was quite clear. She looked sharply up at him, prepared to tell him to mind his own business, but there was something she had not seen in his expression now, and it made her tone down her response.

'What sort of question is that?'

His arms tightened around her. 'Sorry, I didn't mean to sound like an inquisitor. But how do I know what goes as far as you're concerned? You told me you shared a room at college. What did that mean?'

Her voice sharpened. 'You have no earthly right to ask, but I'll tell you. I shared with a girl called Wendy. Okay? And when I say Philip is a friend, I mean just that. I've only just met him, for goodness' sake! Anyway, why the curiosity? This is swinging London, isn't it?'

'No.' Piers' voice was low and caressing and his breath tickled her forehead. 'This isn't swinging London at all. It's you and me, and I want to know where I stand.'

They danced on for a moment in silence, but the mood had changed, quickened into something disturbing.

'Well?' he prompted. 'Where do I stand, Annabel? You haven't answered me.'

'As far as I'm concerned we're having a pleasant night out. A little celebration,' she hedged.

'If I'm having a fun night out, I don't start checking up on my partner's emotional involvement with other people. I'm tired of joking around, Annabel. I'm not a joking kind of person. I'm the kind who knows what he wants.'

'If we're being serious, then I don't think you've known me long enough to be feeling anything more than mild attraction.'

'I've watched you for three years, remember. That's long enough for anything.'

'But I haven't known *you* as long as that, have I?' Why was she arguing with him in this way—as though something more between them was possible, given time?

His hands slid slowly over her silky waist, up her back, pulling her closer against him. 'Of course you haven't. Damn it, I intended being sensible tonight, but all this——' his arms tightened around her '—Annabel, I swear to God you're not indifferent. The feel of you says so, however much you may try to fob me off.'

She gently detached herself from him. 'Let's sit down.'

He pulled out her chair, and when he was seated opposite her he folded his arms on the table, leaning towards her, his eyes holding twin reflections of the candle flame. 'All right, then, let's talk.'

Annabel had thought it would be better here with the width of the table between them and physical contact broken, but it was worse, because there was nowhere to hide, nowhere to look except into the burning intenseness of his face.

So don't hide—attack! she told herself.

'All right, we'll talk. But on my terms.'

She could see him relaxing, confident of winning her over, until her next words wiped the dawn of triumph from his face.

'Let's talk about Kate,' she said.

Piers leaned back, his eyes narrowing, the angular planes of his face thrown into sharp relief as a spotlight on the dance floor caught him momentarily in its beam.

'What is it with you?' he said angrily. 'Why do you keep dragging her into the conversation?'

'She was my friend.'

'*Was.* You said it. It may sound brutal if I emphasise it, Annabel, but what possible relevance has she to you and me now?'

'You asked about Philip, didn't you?'

'He's alive. He could have a part to play in your future. I had to know how you felt about him.'

She looked down at the table, watching the spoon she was nervously turning over and over. 'People don't have to be alive to have an effect—and they're not switched off and out of the way once they're dead. People remember. *I* remember.'

'Damn few people remembered Kate when she was alive,' he countered sharply. 'Where were you all the time she was in London? She never even mentioned you.'

That hurt, but the stab of pain only spurred her on. 'And would it have made a difference to what happened if a friend had been around?'

'Don't twist my words. I was merely stating the obvious—that a friend who won't let her rest in peace was singularly lacking when friendship might have counted for something.' His chair grated sharply on the polished floorboards as he made to rise. 'But if this is what conversation means to you, then I suggest we dance again.'

'Why are you so afraid to explain anything?' Annabel stared up at him defiantly. She was going to stick to her guns this time no matter what happened.

'There's nothing to explain. There was an accident, a tragic accident that robbed the world of a wonderful voice that——'

'A voice! That's all you think about, isn't it, Piers? All you care about is singing and the money you make from it!' Annabel could hardly believe the venom she heard in her own voice. The people at the next table were studiously not looking, but she could sense that they were aware of something going on.

Piers' expression brooked no opposition. 'We'd better leave. This isn't my idea of acceptable public behaviour.'

She modified her voice so that only he could hear. 'And the public view is the all-important one, isn't it? It's all you think about.'

His grip on her arm was iron-hard and she had to snatch

at her handbag to avoid leaving it behind as he whisked her out through the doors into the garden. When they were beyond the glare of the floodlights in the dark shadows of a chestnut tree walk, he pulled her roughly against him and stifled her protesting cry with a kiss that, struggle as she might, she could not get away from.

'This is what I think about, damn you!' he said savagely. 'And this . . . and this . . .' One arm held her while his free hand showed only too explicitly the direction of his thoughts, crushing the silk of her dress and the soft warm flesh beneath it. 'You too . . .' he said urgently, sensing the quick flame that raced through her in defiance of her mind's struggle to remain calm. 'You think about it as well, deny it if you can.'

She willed herself to go limp in his arms, her mouth unresponsive, her hands clenched by her side, and after a moment or two he let her go and met her level accusing gaze.

'Congratulations on the stud performance. Easier than talking, isn't it?' she said scathingly, smoothing down her dress.

Piers stepped back and she saw by the clenching of his jaw in the moonlight that she had reached him. 'I apologise for having blood in my veins. You obviously run on ice.' He shrugged impatiently. 'There doesn't seem much point left in the evening now. I'll take you home.'

'Not until you've told me about Kate.' She stood her ground, though the cold, set look on his face was frightening. 'I want to know what made her so unhappy. I know she was, because she wrote and told me so.'

'Then you know as much as she wanted you to know,' he said curtly. 'And I'm not going any further to satisfy your prurient curiosity. Understand this: my business with you is in the present. I'd like it to extend to the future, but you make it abundantly clear that all you're interested in is ferreting around in the past. *Someone else's* past. If you change your attitude there may be some point in talking. But you're going to have to be the one to change, Annabel. I won't. Shall we go?'

It was better this way, Annabel told herself through the quiet days. She should have had a date with Philip at the weekend—Sunday at the Festival Hall—but at the last moment he rang to cancel for the reason both of them had dreaded. It was a reason that confirmed Annabel's opinion of the sort of man Piers was.

Philip was dropped from the Temple Charing project. His voice had not recovered the expected strength, and he was out, just like that.

Annabel broke her resolve to keep her distance and made a heated phone call to Piers.

'I understand Philip Young isn't with us any more,' she began, her voice ominously tight.

'Yes. Pity, but that's the way it is.'

'Does it *have* to be?' she exploded. 'He's been through a lot for two years, and all the time you've led him to believe he was going to be at Temple Charing.'

'Unfortunately he just isn't going to regain enough strength of voice for opera after his op. He'll be fine on the concert circuit.'

'But that isn't what he wants. Couldn't you at least let him try? What about a less demanding involvement? Minor roles as opposed to leads?'

'And how satisfied do you imagine he'd be with that after

what he's been expecting? I'm sorry, but you must realise that I'm not running a convalescent home. Temple Charing has to be a financially viable project, and as such it needs the best. So it's tough on Philip, but there it is.'

His calm, cold reason inflamed Annabel.

'Are you sure that's the only thing that influenced you?' she said. 'There couldn't be a touch of spite in Philip's omission from the team?'

His voice crackled down the line, making her jump.

'*Never* overestimate your own importance, Annabel,' he snapped. 'When it comes to work one thing and one thing only influences me: excellence. I can nurse no one along out of kindness. And now, before I really lose my temper, I suggest that you kindly concentrate on your own business.'

The phone went down with a bang.

Thank goodness the move to Temple Charing was not far ahead. It would soon be November. 'And once I'm there,' she told herself, 'there'll be so many other people around that Piers Bellingham will never be noticed.'

It was then that she realised that in all likelihood he would not be there at all. Once the project was operating, he would go back to the search for new faces, new talents, and she, along with all the other Temple Charing people, would be a thing of the past. She shrugged disconsolately. It was better that way.

The Barbican Gala, coming at the end of October, took on the nature of a farewell to London. Piers would take her there—he still did that, but these days he booked a taxi for her homeward journey and disappeared once he had checked that all the arrangements were satisfactory.

Annabel was in subdued mood as she dressed for the evening, wearing the white Ariana Blair dress for the first time. She stood looking at herself in the mirror. Lace framed her smooth shoulders and the swell of her breasts. Her eyes were huge in a face that looked tiny against the cloud of dark hair.

If only . . . She could feel the words yearning inside her. If only . . . what? If only Piers had not been the kind of man he was? If only Kate had lived to find someone else . . . someone worthwhile to be happy with? If only what might have been was not ruled out by what was.

The door was open and Piers came straight up to the flat, urbane and devastatingly handsome in his black dinner jacket and pin-tucked shirt.

For the first time since their quarrel he really looked at her, and for a moment his eyes blazed.

'You look . . . quite beautiful,' he said. The light faded as he assessed her appearance for audience effect. 'No jewellery, I see. Good. I think you're right. I hoped this might be an appropriate finishing touch.'

In the dark green box he handed her was a white camellia, its fragrance heady and poignant when she took off the cellophane lid.

'Here, I think.' Piers stood behind her, his arms reaching forward to position the flower to his liking in her hair. 'Yes. It matches what you'll be singing, don't you think?'

Music. It was always music that he thought of. She was singing 'One Fine Day' from *Madam Butterfly*, and it was true that the fragile petals gave an Oriental touch, emphasising the slight slant of her grey eyes. Was it her pride that wanted him to say 'It suits *you*', with no thought of anything else when he looked at her?

He moved back a step or two while she fixed the camellia in place, and in the dimly lit flat with its lights subdued ready for departure, his reflection seemed almost ghost-like. Annabel had the strange feeling that he would always be there symbolically in her mind ... at her shoulder whatever she did, whoever she was with.

She turned to face him and he nodded final approval, then bent and took her hand, raising her fingers to his lips.

'Now we must go,' he said lightly.

He had only been indicating that she was up to performance standard, she thought as she sat beside him in the car, her dress forming a light frothy barrier between them.

At the Barbican he circulated amongst the people in the hospitality room once he had introduced her, and soon it was time for Annabel and the other artists to withdraw to make themselves ready for the night's pereformance. Piers nodded a brief goodbye across the room, and she thought that the gesture would be the last she would see of him.

Walking out on to the platform with the other soloists closed the door on private life for a while, and from that moment Annabel could only think of her work.

The chorus was superb, and the soloists who preceded her made her very aware of the high standard she must reach. She had to sing as she had never sung before.

At last her moment came. She barely heard the speech outlining the aims of the Temple Charing project, or the audience's encouraging applause as she moved forward, a slight ethereal figure in white. Already she was miles away in another land, another culture: Butterfly, living only for the return of her lover, living on hope that must never be allowed to die.

She poured herself into the music, and the concert hall was hushed and intent as she sang, her voice soaring in perfect beauty, matching the intensity and sureness of Butterfly's faith in love.

It was as she took her third bow in acknowledgement of the audience's rapturous acclaim that Annabel became suddenly aware of the tall, dark figure beside the curtain over the exit at the front of the auditorium and her heart gave a sudden lurch. Piers had stayed to hear her after all. She kept her head lowered, glad of the chance to compose herself before looking out over the audience again.

He had not been joining in the tumult of applause. He had been perfectly still, his eyes fixed on her, his face for once not schooled into disciplined control.

'There's something in the way he looks at you . . .' Marta had said, and at the time Annabel had ridiculed the idea, dismissing anything Piers might feel as transient response of any male to any female and nothing more.

But now she had seen what Marta saw, and it wasn't anything to do with passing fancy. That she could easily have coped with. What she had seen on Piers' face in that split second was something infinitely more complex and yet simply unmistakable. It was the look of love.

CHAPTER SEVEN

ANNABEL looked round apprehensively for Piers in the hospitality room afterwards, but he wasn't there. She was profoundly thankful not to have to meet his eyes, wondering whether a shadow of that devastating expression was still lingering there.

This was something she hadn't bargained for. Piers was not supposed to feel the kind of genuine emotion she thought she had seen on his face. He was the eternal predator, the user, the manipulator of people to his own advantage ... not a flesh and blood man with a man's vulnerability.

What now? she wondered as she lay sleepless in her bed. The ground felt to have been violently disturbed beneath her feet. She had an overwhelming desire for the comforting stability of home and resolved to pay her family an unexpected visit.

She found the kitchen table at Lindhurst surrounded by a lively crowd of young people ranging from Sloane Ranger prettiness to bespectacled genius, with her mother beaming at one end and her father at the other, while a giant casserole topped with feather-light dumplings stood waiting to be served.

'What did I say about feeding the five thousand?' Annabel whispered to her mother as they moved up and made room for her on one of the benches.

'Just as well you were right,' her mother replied sweetly, 'or we might have been swanning off to eat out when you turned up out of the blue!'

Later, when they had all dispersed to their separate rooms and her father was giving the lawns the final mowing of the year, Annabel paused in her methodical putting away of the dishes that everybody had helped to stack.

'Mother . . .' she said slowly, 'how do you know about love? Whether it's real or not, I mean. How did you know that Dad loved you?'

Her mother turned a searching look on her. 'And what am I supposed to read into that particular question?'

'Academic interest, for the time being. Go on—answer me.'

'It's a bit of a feat of memory!' Her mother sat down on the bench, frowning in concentration, the tea towel bunched in her lap.

Would I have had to think like this? Annabel wondered, and knew that the answer was no. As long as she lived there was one moment she would never forget.

'I can tell you when!' her mother said triumphantly. 'It was when he turned up at our house with a hamster.'

Annabel burst out laughing.

'No, really, Annabel! My hamster had died and I was very upset. Your father searched the town to find another one with almost exactly the same markings, then he brought it over on two buses in a shopping bag. He didn't like hamsters one little bit, actually, and mine had bitten him more than once, so I knew he was serious about me. As far as I was concerned, I think I really knew I loved him when he told me he had the chance of a job in Australia. I hadn't the least doubt that I would follow him to Timbuktu rather than lose him. I just couldn't imagine life with him not around.'

'I see . . .' Annabel was staring out of the window thoughtfully. Well, that let her out. She was glad she was

leaving London. And after last night doubly glad that Piers
Bellingham with all his complications wouldn't be featur-
ing in her life for much longer.

'Is "I see" all I'm getting out of you?' her mother
prompted.

'It is for the moment.' Annabel turned round and planted
a kiss on her mother's nose. 'I'll tell you the minute there's
something nice to tell, honestly. There's nothing to hush up
at the moment.' She darted about doing the last bits of
clearing up as she spoke. 'Now, what are we going to do?
Any jobs? Or do you want to go for a walk?'

'We'll have a walk while the sun's out if you like, but
before you go back I'd be glad if you'd sort out your college
papers. They're still in the corner of our bedroom. We can
put them in the attic if there's nothing you need for the
moment.'

It was late in the afternoon when Annabel started on her
files and folders and the stack of miscellaneous objects she
had pushed into carrier bags, too tired to go through them
all at the end of term. There didn't seem to be anything she
would want at Temple Charing, and much of the contents
of the carrier bags could be thrown away.

Suddenly she stopped, a sharp stab of recognition
freezing her fingers. There, tucked into the pages of a
December magazine two years old—why had she kept it so
long?—was Kate's last letter.

Annabel smoothed it out. There was an address printed
at the top of the page. Kate had obviously used someone's
private stationery. It was turning chilly in the bedroom
with the central heating not yet on, but as Annabel's eyes
strained against the fading light, the cold that reached
down and spread its icy fingers came from deep inside her.

The address printed in tiny italics was Piers' address.
Kate had written from his house. That meant only one

thing: she must have been living with him. What else could it mean?

Annabel sank back on her heels while the knowledge ate into her mind, confirmed by what she went on to read.

'Piers says he will never marry me'—those were the familiar words, the ones she had never forgotten, but after them came the words that had only made a vague impression two years ago but were now so clear an exposition of Piers' callousness. 'All he cares about is music. Women are a negligible, disposable feature in his life. Anyone will do to suit the need of the moment, and anything more permanent would be an undesirable millstone round his neck. That's what I am—undesirable. Why was I ever such a fool as to believe I could be anything more? But he *did* make me think that, once.'

No more room for doubt. The evidence was here that Piers had played around with Kate as long as it suited him, totally unconcerned about what happened to her afterwards.

Oh . . . Annabel curled over until her head rested on her knees. He was despicable. How could he have watched what was happening to Kate and not care? What kind of man would be a passive spectator of another human being's disintegration? No wonder he didn't want to talk about it!

Her hands clenched in impotent rage. She wanted to make him pay. No one should get away with what he had done. It grew dark as she sat there, her mind circling round and round. She kept seeing the way he had looked at her last night, then his face would change to an evil expression of scorn. So persistent was the image that she eventually began to feel that the answer must be there.

Supposing she used this feeling Piers had for her now—transient though it must be—and turned it against him? Suppose that just for once, when he thought he was about to get her, something that he believed in his grasp should be snatched away from him?

A tiny thrill of excitement stirred deep down inside Annabel. Yes, that was the answer, she was sure. But footsteps along the corridor sent the tendril of excitement curling back on itself to wait, biding its time.

She was getting stiffly to her feet when the door opened and her mother appeared, switching on the light.

'Why on earth are you working in the dark, love?' she queried. 'Tea's ready. You must be frozen!' She stooped to feel the cold hands Annabel had been oblivious of. 'Come along, now—the fire's lovely in the sitting-room, and I've done pikelets. Doesn't that make you think of winter?'

'Winter . . . yes, it does.' But winter could be inside you, colder than anything the season could bring forth.

Fortunately there was plenty her parents wanted to ask her, and the 'busyness' of tea round the fire covered up Annabel's preoccupation to some extent. Below the surface, beneath the question-answering, though, her plan was hardening, shaping itself, beginning to burn inside her.

'Are you sure you've nothing on your mind?' her mother asked anxiously before Annabel left.

'Nothing more than a little nervousness about Temple Charing. I'm going to have to prove myself against competition there, you know.'

'You'll be fine, of course you will!' Her father's confidence in her was unshakable. 'And see that we get invited to what you're doing, won't you? We don't want a repetition of the Barbican business.' He had been bitterly disappointed not to have tickets to such a big concert.

'That won't happen again,' she told him. 'My inclusion in the programme came after all the seats had been sold, that's all. They were very sorry.'

'Not half as sorry as we were!' He gave her a bone-crushing hug. 'Take care, love.'

They had no idea, Annabel thought as she said goodbye to them, how much she would need to take care over the coming weeks. She was about to embark on a very dangerous game indeed, and a man like Piers Bellingham was the last person to play dangerous games with. However, she had decided what to do, and now she must set about doing it.

She flung her red scarf defiantly round her neck as she came out of the station at Richmond, and made straight for Nightingale Lane.

The house was in darkness apart from the sitting-room. The curtains were open, revealing the glow of lamps, and she could hear the faint sound of Mozart—the Sinfonia Concertante.

Annabel gave in to the temptation and tiptoed across the grass to peep in. If he had company, then now was not the time for what she intended doing.

No . . . he was alone. He was sitting opposite the window, legs stretched out lazily, head resting back on the cushions of the settee, his eyes closed as he listened to the music. He was not sleeping, she could tell, because one of the fingers of the hand resting on the arm of the settee was tapping in time to the music. He looked relaxed, peaceful. Her lips tightened grimly. He didn't know what was coming to him!

She moved back to the door and pulled the old-fashioned bell-pull. Footsteps came quickly towards the door and it opened, letting a dazzling pool of light fall on her face.

'Annabel! Is anything wrong?' His initial smile at seeing her was chased by quick concern.

'No, nothing at all,' she said quietly. 'I just wanted to talk to you.'

'How very nice. Come in. Let me take your coat.'

He laid it on a chair in the hall and showed her into the sitting-room.

'Sit down. Let me turn the settee round to the fire.'

Quite by chance she sat where he had been sitting, and his warmth was still there in the cushions, transferring itself to her own body through the fine wool of her skirt.

'May I get you a drink? You look cold.' Piers touched her cheek with the back of his hand and she welcomed the sharp sensation that ran through her at the feel of his fingers. Good. It was good that he could make her feel something—she would be all the more convincing when she did what she had come to do. If her mind and her body hated him equally, it would be impossible.

'I've been home for the day, and I walked up from the station,' she told him. 'The pavements were sparkling with frost—far too early.'

'Would you prefer something hot, then?'

'No. If you've got whisky and ginger, that would be fine.' Fine for bolstering her courage, but he was not to know that.

While he was busy at the drinks table, she looked round the room that had been too crowded at the party for her to really see it. There were watercolours on the white walls, and the elaborate Victorian plasterwork on the ceiling was picked out in pastels that mirrored the gentle colours of the Indian carpet. Peacock-blue velvet curtains echoed the fabric of the settees and chairs, and gold lampshades cast pools of soft, mellow light. It was a room to lull the senses, a deceptively peaceful room to blind whoever entered it to the true nature of its owner.

'Here you are.' Piers handed her a crystal tumbler and stooped to poke the log fire into blazing life, then he sat down in an easy chair opposite the settee, watching her, his face betraying nothing more than polite curiosity as to why she was there.

The whisky burned a fierce path of courage down her throat. Annabel put the glass carefully on the coffee table in front of her and prepared to speak.

'Shall I turn this off?' He had already lowered the volume of the stereo.

'No, don't. It's lovely. One of my favourite bits of Mozart.' Hardly music to practise deception by, she thought uncomfortably.

'So. What was it that brought you here so unexpectedly at this time of day—not that I'm complaining.'

She edged forward on the cushions. 'I came to apologise.'

There was suddenly tension in his stillness: an awareness that things were on the point of change.

'Go on . . .' he said slowly. 'I'm not sure what you're talking about. As I recollect, the last time I saw you at the Barbican was an occasion for triumph, not apology.'

She looked up and met his eyes. 'Oh yes, you do know, Piers. I'm apologising for the way I ruined that lovely evening at Giulietta's. It was wrong of me to keep on at you as I did. I don't know what got into me. It was unpardonable.'

His expression had not changed at all. He didn't show any of the signs she had been expecting. She wasn't convincing him. She looked desperately down at her hands, tightly clenched in her lap.

'So humble, Annabel?' There was faint mockery in his voice. 'Forgive me if I find this side of you less credible than the fierce little vixen who bit the hand that fed her!'

'I've said I'm sorry, and I meant it.'

'Yes—but why? Why the sudden U-turn? It is one, isn't it?'

She drew in a trembling breath. 'I find it hard to

apologise. I'm not doing this very well.'

'I'm not hurrying you. You can take all night if you like.'

Annabel shot a quick glance at him then. He was staring at her, his eyes keen and challenging. How could she bring back that look she'd seen on his face at the Barbican—the look that was essential to her purpose? Come as close to the truth as she could? Yes, that way she was bound to be more real.

'Maybe I'd better be completely honest. I'm still—I mean—what was worrying me then is still of importance. But I was wrong to make it an issue affecting you and me. I—I don't want anything to come between us.'

'You mean you don't think it politic to quarrel with someone as much involved with your career as I am?'

'No!' she exploded in hot denial. Piers' face was still a carefully sculpted mask of polite scepticism. She was getting nowhere. Was she making a complete fool of herself in thinking he had any feelings at all for her?

'Then you thought you might have hurt my feelings, perhaps? Believe me, Annabel, I haven't reached where I am through excessive sensitivity!'

She could feel the situation slipping away from her.

'So——' He sat forward suddenly in his chair, startling her. 'Having got that little misunderstanding out of the way, let's take it that all is forgiven. Drink your whisky.'

She picked up her glass, playing for time. 'Could I have a little more ginger, please?' She couldn't—she simply couldn't let it all fizzle out like this. She could fake emotion on stage and reduce an audience to tears. She could create a love-crazed Butterfly, knowing all the time that Pinkerton was a rat . . . so why couldn't she come up with the goods now? She *had* to do it.

She was standing up when Piers turned round with her topped-up glass. She took it from him determinedly and put it down at once, her free hand restraining him from going back to his chair.

'This is what I didn't want anything to spoil . . .' she said, her voice husky and shy as she stood on tiptoe to press her lips to his. It was a gesture of instinct, not of rational thought, and instinct made her hands slide round his neck, her body cling to his.

What had begun in pretence became something that it was not in her power to control as her mind and body seemed to move into another plane with dimensions so vast, so dazzling, that she could only let herself float into them.

She felt his hands come up slowly to span her slender rib cage, and at their touch her heart beat such a frantic tattoo that she had to gasp for breath.

He held her away from him then, and his dark eyes looked searchingly into hers.

'Well now . . .' he said softly, 'here's a thing . . .' His voice was questioning as he scanned her face as though for proof that he was not dreaming.

Then he took the initiative, his mouth tasting her soft lips, his breath one with hers, his arms moulding her body to his.

Why, it's easy! Annabel thought wonderingly in the first split second. I can do it! I can make myself think it's real, think that I really mean it. Then for a while there was no room for thought, only for the explosion of sensation that possessed her, making her aware of her body in a way she had never before experienced.

The slow withdrawal of his lips from hers brought her spiralling earthwards again, and she raised her lashes with a sense of bemused wonder to find herself in the real world.

Piers' dark eyes gleamed between narrowed lids.

'A little more of this and I'll be absolutely convinced,' he said, his voice husky and breathless, his long fingers lifting her hair and crushing it sensuously as he buried his face in its fragrant silkiness.

He raised his head suddenly, becoming aware of their exposure to passing eyes beyond the dark windows.

'Don't go away . . .' He kissed the tip of her nose, then gently released her to go over and pull the curtains. 'Now, start convincing me again.'

Annabel stared down at the carpet, her hair drooping forward, sure that his face would be mocking her.

'You're making fun of me.' Her voice trembled over the words.

He tilted her chin up so that she was forced to look at him.

'Oh no, I'm not . . .' he said, and it was there again, the look she had seen on his face at the Gala, its impact more shattering than ever with his eyes so close to hers, blazing with a fire that made her want to step back and yet at the same time to melt into his arms again.

Now what was going to happen? She had a momentary fit of panic. This was too quick, suddenly, this drawing of the curtains, this being enclosed in the warm privacy of his house with him looking at her like that. She wanted time—time to wind him up to such a degree that her rejection of him—and oh yes! she was going to reject him—so that it bruised his ego as it had never been bruised before.

What he did both surprised and momentarily relieved her. He kissed her gently on each lowered eyelid, then pulled her down beside him on the settee and settled her head comfortably on his shoulder, seeming disposed to take things gently.

'Now let's talk,' he said. 'Tell me what made you change your mind.'

She gave a little sigh of relief. 'It was the thought of going away up to Temple Charing . . . of not seeing you again. I didn't want it to end with you being angry with me. It seemed so stupid. What's past should be over and done with.' Her fingers played with the gold strap on his watch.

'Then I'm glad . . .' He kissed the top of her head. 'But you'll not be leaving me, you know. I'll be there too—at least until the end of the Company's first season.'

The unexpectedness of that made her stiffen in surprise. She had thought there was little more than a week, but the field was open for much longer. This needed thinking about.

'You're not going back on what you said, are you?' His fingers tightened round her shoulder. 'If there's any threat of that we'll stop talking right away and go back to something that doesn't leave room for misunderstanding.'

Annabel rubbed her face into the soft cashmere of his sweater.

'Of course I'm not going back on anything. I was just surprised—wonderfully surprised. I can't believe you'll be there too. I was so sure your job would end when we left London.'

'Not a bit of it. I have to audition the chorus in the Midlands so that they can be largely home-based and cut costs. Oh, my dear, sweet love! There's masses to arrange up there. Performances at Temple Charing are only the half of it. You'll be going out into the community presenting opera where it's never been seen and heard before: schools, factories, parks, colleges, stately homes— everywhere! There's enough to keep me busy for several months. Oh no, you're not going to lose me.' His voice deepened and his grip tightened. 'And I'm certainly not going to let you escape. To prove it: what's it going to be? Rubies, emeralds, sapphires, diamonds? The lot?'

She panicked and pulled away from him. 'What do you mean?'

'The ring, of course. It's not unusual in such cases, I believe?'

'But you didn't say—I didn't think—we never——'

Piers shook her gently. 'Stop stammering! I've been around long enough to know that when the object of my desires at last shows signs of the same inclination, it's time to get down to serious plans. We're making a firm commitment to each other as of this very moment.'

Keep it close to reality ... Play it as straight as you can ... Annabel's fevered mind told her. What good reason could you have, in all seriousness, for reservations?

'Oh, Piers!' She turned her head to kiss him on the corner of his mouth. 'I want to ... I really do. But is it a good idea to let other people in on our secret?' She silenced an attempted protest with another kiss. 'No—really. Just imagine—they're all going to say I only got the job because there was something going on between us. Oh, forgive me for being selfish, but I don't want it to look like that. Can't we hold back for just a little longer—just until I've proved myself under my own flag?'

His finger traced the shape of her face, then ran across the furrows of the anxious frown on her forehead.

'What an independent, proud little creature you are! But maybe that's part of what draws me to you.' He took his arm away from her shoulders, leaving them feeling strangely bare. 'I think I know something that can stand in for a ring until you feel ready for the real thing. Wait here.'

Well, Annabel thought while she drew breath—he hadn't argued, had he? He almost seemed too willing to keep things quiet. What if he was doing what she was doing—playing a game, pretending, but for different reasons? He wanted passing amusement achieved by any means, just as she wanted revenge. A double-sided game ... What would she achieve under those circumstances?

He wasn't gone long. When he came back he sat down beside her again and opened a small, worn, wine-coloured velvet box on her lap. He took out a locket, oval and finely chased, on a thick Victorian chain. His face was strangely serious as he opened it, revealing two tiny portraits of women. One was sepia, faded and obviously very old, the face sweetly solemn with its smooth twenties hairstyle, the slender neck rising from a square neckline.

'My grandmother,' he said. 'Cornelia Bellingham. And this was my mother, Helen. She died when I was at Oxford. For some reason her illness was kept from me until it was too late. Her death they couldn't conceal.'

Annabel didn't need to look at his face to see how bad that time had been. The pain of it was still in his voice after how many years? Ten at the very least.

'She was lovely. They both were,' she said, and the relief of speaking the plain truth was overwhelming. The dark eyes of Piers' mother had the steady directness of his, and the fine, narrow features were a softened, feminine version of his own.

He opened the right-hand side of the locket and she saw that his mother's picture was on a hinged central piece which revealed two empty ovals.

'Room for two more Bellingham women,' he said. 'You—and maybe our daughter before very long, if I have my way.'

Annabel couldn't have spoken then for worlds, but the gentle, lingering kiss he gave her removed the necessity.

'Let me put it on for you,' he said.

'It—it's very precious. Such a family thing for you to give away so lightly.'

'Not lightly. I want it to show you the measure of my feelings for you. Hold your hair up.'

She did as he asked and he clasped the locket round her

throat, kissing the nape of her neck as he did so, then he
pulled her round to face him and dropped the locket down
inside her jumper where it lay like a hot coal from hell
against her flesh. Her eyes filled with sudden tears.

He was genuine. She had to believe it. Nobody could do
that, sound like that, and not mean it.

'I don't know what to say, Piers.'

'We've said what matters. We know what we mean to
each other. If the world has to wait a while, so be it. All
right, now?'

She nodded dumbly. She had the strangest sensation that
his voice was winding its way down inside her until it
touched the most painful, raw nerve her body possessed.

Are you satisfied now? she asked herself when she was back
at Marta's getting ready for bed. Are you pleased with
what you're doing?

The locket gleamed between her breasts, and her eyes
were drawn in reluctant fascination to its reflection in the
mirror.

When she had embarked on this revenge—and a shabby
business it was beginning to seem—it had been her against
him, in isolation. She hadn't pictured him as part of a
loving family—a family that cared and remembered, a
family that handed things down from one generation to
another. Her picture of him had shifted now, moved into an
area that made it hard to regard him as a straightforward
target for contempt.

She struggled for control of her feelings. Kate had a
family, she told herself roughly. That's the one you must
keep in mind. No going back. You're in this now. You'll see
it through, and if you don't enjoy it, so much the better. You
promised yourself an easing of conscience, not a picnic.

Words were not enough, though. Feelings scored

inexorably. Her body could recall Piers' touch, her eyes his eyes, her mind his words.

She flung herself on to the bed and cried, but there was no relief in the tears. They only made the pillow wet.

As though by deliberate intent, a shaft of moonlight fell on the locket where it lay on the bedside table. Impatiently she turned over, and the dressing-table mirror tossed the reflection scornfully in her face. She closed her eyes, but still she knew it was there.

CHAPTER EIGHT

'TEARS, Annabel? On an exciting day like this?'

Annabel managed a wobbly smile for Marta and Sylvia. She had called in to say goodbye to them. Any time now the minibus coming down from Temple Charing to pick up the Young Opera Group people from London would arrive, and the lovely hours spent over lessons in Marta's drawing-room would be over.

She was sad for that reason, but her tendency to dissolve into tears owed more to the confusion that had built up in her over the past days. Piers had not put a foot wrong. He had been charming, understanding, loving . . . She wanted to believe it wouldn't last—that once he got what he wanted he would add her to his score card and move on, but damn him! he gave the best impression of sincerity she had ever come across.

Kissing him goodnight—kissing him any time—was no problem at all. The problem was rapidly coming to be in the area of stopping kissing him. She groped angrily in her pocket for a handkerchief. How could she be thinking like this. It was contemptible. She had these extremes of emotion warring inside her, and sometimes it seemed anybody's guess which would win.

'Here!' Marta thrust a tissue into her hand. 'Stop this before I join you.' She watched while Annabel mopped up. 'You're going to be very happy at Temple Charing, you know. Really you are!'

Annabel gulped and attempted another smile. 'Yes, of course I am. But it's been so wonderful here, Marta. I've learned so much, and I'm going to miss you. I can never thank you enough.'

'You can thank me by being successful—and by enjoying every minute on stage just as I did.' A roguish smile flickered across the singer's face. 'And if you remember anything else that would please me, feel free to do it!'

Before Annabel could work that out there was a crunch of wheels on the gravel and the double blast of a horn. Sylvia ran over to the window.

'They're here. We'll come down and wave you off. Marta, put this round your shoulders.' She picked up the mohair shawl on the arm of the chair and knotted it solicitously, then together they all three went downstairs.

'Good job you're the last one!' the driver commented as he stowed Annabel's luggage in the crowded compartment.

She gave Marta and Sylvia a final hug, then climbed on board to a chorus of greetings, and stood waving from the doorway as the bus moved off.

Hugh signalled from the back where he was sitting with Selwyn Burman, Philip's replacement, and patted the seat in front of them, but Vivienne was nearer.

'I've kept a place for you,' she called, and Annabel couldn't walk on by. Since she didn't feel much like talking it didn't matter who was her travelling companion.

She slipped into the seat, noting wryly that even for an early bus ride Vivienne was dressed to kill. Soft violet coat and leggings . . . white frothy blouse spilling over a brocade waistcoat . . . No need to wonder who thought she was the company's number one!

'How are you, Vivienne?'

'As well as this ungodly hour encourages anyone to be,' she answered. 'Glad to be getting on with things at last, though, aren't you?'

'Yes ... but sorry in a way that this bit's over.'

'I thought you might be.' She slanted an odd, knowing look which Annabel was at a loss to interpret. 'You've been having pretty special treatment, haven't you?'

'It's been wonderful. There was nothing at college to compare with the past weeks.'

'I'll *bet* there wasn't! Are you going to tell me about it?' Vivienne glanced at her tiny gold watch. 'You've got two hours at least for a blow-by-blow account.'

'About Marta Kane?' Annabel was puzzled. Vivienne must have been having similar tuition, surely? Philip certainly had been.

'Of course not! I can see you're going to be a dab hand at fobbing off the press when you want to. But I don't "fob off" so easily. Try again.'

'You mean the Barbican, then?' There was something in Vivienne's voice that was beginning to worry her. Was she jealous that she hadn't been chosen for the Gala? Was this the first taste of unpleasant atmospheres to come?

'No! Not the Barbican, you crafty thing. I want to know about Piers. About *you* and Piers. Is that clear enough for you?'

Undoubtedly it was. Clear enough to stop the circulation, in fact. So much for refusing to travel up with Piers to avoid speculation! Annabel made a mammoth attempt to compose herself.

'Sorry,' she said, 'I'm still lost. It's early in the day for me too. I don't really function properly before noon.'

Vivienne's green eyes didn't waver. 'Then let me tell you

a little story to help you wake up. One Sunday—a week last Sunday, to be exact—a friend whose identity doesn't matter cooked me a meal at his flat. At Richmond. Richmond where you live . . . and Piers. Afterwards we had a long walk by the river and back down Richmond Hill. We happened to pass Piers' house, where we saw a charming little vignette through the window.'

The pause dragged on interminably. What? Oh, what had they seen? Slowly, tantalisingly, Vivienne went on.

'Piers was just coming across the room to draw the curtains. And you—you were looking very pretty and maidenly, waiting for whatever happened next that we couldn't see. I wonder what that could have been?'

She was like a cat with a mouse. Annabel played for time. 'Oh—*that* evening.'

'Yes, *that* evening. Come on, now. Give!'

'There's nothing to give . . . really.' How much had she seen? How long before the drawing of the curtains? A minute would be enough to make the picture very clear. If she really had seen more, though, wouldn't she have said so? It was worth bluffing a bit longer. 'Oh, I remember now,' Annabel went on. 'Piers wanted to talk over the Barbican concert with me. There wasn't time the night before, and I'd been home all day Sunday, so he asked me to call in on my way back. Nothing more interesting than that, I'm afraid.'

'Really?' Vivienne looked sceptical. 'I know Piers, remember, and there's a lot of heat below that oh-so-cool exterior.'

'Is there? It sounds as though you know more about it than I do.'

'Maybe. Maybe not. I can zip up too, sweetie.' She

turned to look out of the window.

Checkmate? It looked like it. Annabel wasn't quite reassured, but she gave sigh of relief for temporary reprieve as they went on to safer topics: topics in which Vivienne Blake was the centre pin around which the conversation revolved.

Oxfordshire gave way to Gloucestershire, and soon the driver called over his shoulder that they were nearly there. The babble of conversation died down as everyone began to look around with heightened interest and the minibus swung between high Cotswold stone gateposts into a long, tree-lined drive.

'What price slipping out to the nearest chemist's with all this distance to walk?' Vivienne complained, then the house itself came into view. It was a sprawling, mellow building that seemed to have grown out of the golden landscape. They had barely time to notice smooth lawns and a glimpse of a lake ahead before the bus swerved round the back and into a courtyard where Annabel could see Piers' car parked along with several others.

Don't let him single me out, she prayed hurriedly as she gathered her things together and prepared to file out with the others. Vivienne's sharp green eyes would be watching, she knew, ready to spot the slightest hint of anything special in the way he behaved towards her.

When she saw his tall figure coming out of the house, elegant in fawn polo-necked sweater and slacks, she turned to speak to Hugh, her pulse racing. A surreptitious sideways glance showed that Piers was his usual calm, authoritative self.

'Leave your big luggage in the bus,' he told them, 'And come to the canteen. We'll sort out where you're all going to be, then you can collect your cases before you go and settle in.'

They followed him in an excited, chattering bunch, through a side door in the courtyard and along a corridor to the canteen, a former coach-house, he told them, where everyone was provided with coffee.

'And now if you'll all bring your cups to this end, I'd like to say a few words about accommodation and general procedure.' Piers perched on a table at the front of the room as he spoke, and they all gathered round him.

'This is where we find out what causes us to get our fingers slapped,' Hugh said wickedly. 'Come on, sit up straight and look good!'

Now at last Annabel could justifiably look at Piers as everyone else was doing. She needn't have worried about him. He didn't by the slightest flicker of an eye or lingering glance betray anything. But then why should that surprise her? Covering up was his skill, wasn't it?

She listened while he told them the general layout of the house and its outbuildings and grounds, using a plan on the canteen wall. The Opera House was behind and slightly to the right of the main house, linked to it by a covered walkway, and the audience would be served drinks in the main hall, he told them, before walking through the garden to the performance.

'Your meals will be served in here,' he went on. 'Breakfast will be self-service, so that you can have it or not according to inclination. The same applies at weekends, incidentally, and you'll all be required to notify catering staff on Friday morning as to whether or not you will be here on Saturday and Sunday.'

'They let us out! Modified freedom! One degree better

than the army!' Hugh's low aside made Annabel smile, then straighten her face guiltily as Piers caught her doing it.

'We're a bit isolated, Piers. How many miles is it to the nearest bit of civilisation, for goodness' sake?' Vivienne's blonde head tilted appealingly as she looked up at him.

'There *is* public transport outside London, strange as it may seem, Vivienne,' he told her. 'And in addition to the regular bus service we intend running the mini-bus into Cirencester on one weekday, and Cheltenham on Saturday. That should do something to satisfy your craving for the bright lights.'

'It's not just that. We have appearances to keep up—but I suppose you men will never understand that.' She pouted prettily, but to no avail, for Piers was already turning away.

'And now I expect you're all wanting to see your rooms. Accommodation varies, but I think you'll all find you have everything you need. If not, let me know. I shan't be actually staying on the estate, but I shall be in most days, and my office is here in the Opera House block. Now, eight of you will be in the stable block—here.' He pointed out the situation on the map.

'Stables!' Tessa clapped her hand to her mouth too late to stifle the exclamation, then ducked her head to hide behind her long red hair.

Piers grinned. 'Don't worry, all traces of horses have been removed. So—Mark, David, Shona, Andy, Charles, Liz, Cathy and Tessa—here are your keys. Check where to go on the plan.'

There was an excited milling around for a few moments before he could continue. 'Hugh and Selwyn, you're in the courtyard where the bus dropped you—flatlets at the far end facing the house. Separate ones, so that you don't sing each other to death.' He tossed keys to each of them.

'Annabel, you're in the back lodge, at the end of the rear drive. You'll find that beyond the Opera House. And Vivienne, you have this cottage here at the end of the lake : formerly the gardener's. It's set back a little in a spinney.'

'Favouritism!' someone called out.

'Logic,' countered Piers. 'Main soloists need a certain isolation for private practice.'

'And how!' another voice replied with feeling and there was general laughter.

'Right, off you go to inspect your quarters, then. Lunch will be at one, here. Briefing in the Opera House at three this afternoon. Right—David? Charles? Anything to add?' The producer and musical director shook their head, and the party began to break up.

Vivienne had gone over to the plan and caught up with Annabel on the way out of the canteen.

'Have you noticed,' she began sweetly, 'that your lodge is on the road, well away from the rest of us?'

'Lodges usually are on roads,' Annabel said shortly, guessing what was coming.

'But wouldn't it be convenient if anyone wanted to visit you? I mean, they could just pop in and out again, and no on would be any the wiser. It wouldn't be so easy for the rest of us, would it?'

'I expect we could do a swop if you feel you could make more use of that facility than I shall.' Annabel stared boldly into the mocking green eyes and saw them waver momentarily.

'Heavens, no! I should hate to risk incurring Piers' wrath . . . by messing about with his arrangements, I mean. I'm sure he thought it all out very carefully.'

'Vivienne—Annabel——' They turned round as Piers called their names, both starting guiltily. 'Put your cases in the boot of my car. I'll drop them off for you and risk talk of favouritism again. It isn't far, but a couple of cases make a difference.'

'We were just wondering why you'd chosen to isolate the pair of us,' said Vivienne, pointing out her luggage and leaving Piers to deal with it while Annabel lugged her own things over to his car and stood waiting for him to open the boot.

'I could have put you both in the courtyard flats, but there's marginally less room there, and since women have such a load of possessions I thought I'd give you the cottages. Let me know if you find the distance a problem.'

His back was to Vivienne and he gave Annabel a solemn wink as he took her cases from her. That was the only brief personal acknowledgement he made. With exemplary tact, he dropped her off first before going on round the lake with Vivienne.

The lodge was deceptively roomy inside. The door opened straight into the main room, bright with oatmeal carpet and rose-patterned chintz covers on the chairs. The kitchen was large enough to have a small table in a bay which had been built out into the garden so that the effect was of eating out of doors, and the bedroom and bathroom were both pleasant and cheerful with modern furniture and fittings, and matching almond-green colour schemes. There was a telephone, connected, in the living-room.

The road Annabel could see from the kitchen window was hardly more than a lane and the drive gates were padlocked and rather rusty, so it looked as though she would not be disturbed unless by intent. She remembered Vivienne's words and frowned. It wasn't going to be easy to shut her up, and the last thing Annabel wanted was gossip among the others. She would have to keep a very low profile.

The obvious disadvantage of that was how on earth to keep Piers' interest on the boil if she was scared to speak to him. Oh, the sooner the silly business was over, the better. But there were the chorus auditions and all those bookings he had talked about to arrange. Hell! How was she going to cope?

Unpacking her things and walking briskly up to the canteen for lunch occupied her mind a little more satisfactorily. Piers spent the lunch hour in a huddle with David and Charles, and it was easy for Annabel to relax under the zany influence of Hugh and Selwyn.

After lunch, Piers disappeared and for Annabel her first sight of the Opera House left no room for thoughts of anything other than the enormous thrill of working in such a place. With the others she stood on the huge, empty stage, then wandered round backstage through dressing-rooms, wardrobe, offices and scenery store. Sets for the two opening productions were already being constructed in the workshops behind the main house, John told them, and he showed them scale models for each change of scene. Tessa had pinned up sketches of her costume designs, and fixed a time for a measuring session the following morning, after which she and her two assistants would begin work on their mammoth task of dressing two productions.

Charles took over and explained his interpretation of the two operas, then when the briefing ended and gave way to general chatter Annabel wandered back on to the stage, drawn by its waiting magnetism. She looked out over the banked rows of velvet seats, imagining the heavy folds of the red and gold curtains moving silently across the footlights with that exciting rush of air.

It was all becoming solid and real—so real that what was going on between her and Piers seemed doubly false in this setting. A play within a play—like *Hamlet*. But *Hamlet* was a tragedy, wasn't it? She shivered, and was glad when the others burst on stage from the wings with comic over-dramatic entrances.

That night, after dinner, they all went down to West Haston, the nearest village, and found a pub called The Lamb where they spent a couple of hours before walking home along the quiet roads in the moonlight, linking arms, and the whole crowd going noisily round the grounds at Temple Charing seeing first Annabel and then Vivienne safely settled before going back to their own more central quarters.

Piers had disappeared immediately after the meal, and with him the tension Annabel felt. It could be good there, she thought sleepily, still cheered by the sense of comradeship as she lay in bed. She would like it, once everything was settled.

She had only just got out of bed next morning when there was a sharp tap on the door.

'Who is it?' She hesitated before turning the key, rapidly slipping on her dressing-gown and fastening the belt.

'Me.' The deep voice was unmistakable.

Hurriedly she opened the door and Piers stepped inside, smiling and elegant in a fine grey tweed suit. Annabel was piqued at the contrast between them.

'What are you doing here at this time?'

'This, to begin with.' He pulled her towards him and kissed her. 'You're all warm and sleepy. Have you only just got up?'

'I should think so! It's barely seven o'clock. What are you *doing* here, Piers?'

'I've come to breakfast. I might make quite a habit of it. I've got to be able to get near you without putting on an act some time.'

'But what if you're seen?'

'Who's going to see me at this time of day? Nobody's likely to surface much before nine when the canteen opens, if then.' He reached for her again. 'You've no idea how much I wanted to do this yesterday. It took a fair bit of willpower to ignore you, I can tell you.'

She pulled away and looked anxiously out of the window. 'Where's your car?'

'Further down the lane in a side road. Credit me with some sense, Annabel!' He sat down, pulling her on to his knees, and she subsided against him with a shamefaced smile.

'I was longing to talk to you,' she told him. 'I couldn't think how on earth we were going to get any time at all together.'

'I've got it all worked out. I shall go back to the car—eventually—drive it around to the main entrance, park, and be in my office at nine with nobody any the wiser.'

Annabel's anxiety came back. 'I wouldn't be too sure of that. Vivienne gave me quite a bad time yesterday on the way here. Piers, don't *do* that!'

He wasn't concentrating. He was getting far too interested in the buttons on her dressing-gown. She grabbed his hands and held them.

'I can do two things at once. Tell me about Vivienne.' He freed one hand, neatly imprisoned both of hers in an iron grip, and proceeded to demonstrate.

Annabel couldn't speak. She had only to feel his touch on her skin and she wanted to forget everything . . . just put her arms round him, hide her face in his neck, and ignore the whole world. The awful contrast between how she was supposed to feel and how she actually did feel overwhelmed her. The tremendous difficulty of sticking to the scheme she had cooked up suddenly towered over her like some impossible killer mountain. She didn't want to make Piers suffer. She didn't want to believe he'd done what he had to Kate. She didn't want to remember anything—just start again from now with no past, no deception.

'O-o-o-h!' She pulled away from him with a stifled sob.

'Annabel!' Now at least she had his attention. 'What is it? What did that hell-cat do to upset you like this?'

Vivienne . . . yes, hang on to that. Make yourself believe that Vivienne is the only thing wrong with your world.

'She saw us in your house, the night you gave me the locket.' Her hand went up to touch it; she only took it off in the bath. 'She didn't see much, but enough to set her thinking. She'll talk to the others, Piers.'

'What on earth was she doing round Nightingale Lane?' He didn't really care, she could tell. He was just curious.

'Does it matter? She was there, and she saw.'

'It matters to you.'

'You know why.' Childishly she wiped her eyes on her sleeve and he laughed at her.

'Oh, my love, how difficult you make your life! All we need do is let it be known how things really are between us.

If everyone knew we were far more than working colleagues, we could meet as often as we liked and nobody would have anything to talk about.'

'You know why I don't want to do that,' Annabel said petulantly, angry at the way he simplified a situation about whose complexity he had no idea.

He kissed the frown off her forehead and the downward turn from her lips. 'Then the other alternative that occurs to me is for me to keep dear Vivienne busy so that she's no time for speculation.'

She didn't understand immediately. She thought he meant work. 'You mean extra rehearsals or something?'

He grinned and tweaked her nose. 'I mean that I could take her out . . .' Annabel went dangerously still, '. . . wine and dine her a bit. She'll soon cook up a whole new scenario in that little blonde head of hers.'

'And wouldn't you just enjoy helping her do it while she flaunts herself in her down-to-the-ankles necklines!' Searing jealousy at the thought of him with Vivienne swept her from petulance to boiling rage, rage that was instantly doubled by exasperation with herself for feeling it.

Piers looked at her with that dark, level look. 'If we're thinking of it from my point of view I'd sooner have you, modestly smothered in an old blue dressing-gown, than anything Vivienne displays on a help-yourself basis. But we're not talking about me, are we? You're the reason for it all, Annabel. I'm only going along with this silly cloak and dagger business because you want it. I couldn't care less if we rushed out of here this very second and told the whole world we were going to be married.'

'I'm sorry. I know you're right. I'm just finding it all more complicated than I ever dreamed.' She snuggled back against him. If she went on like this she'd be the biggest turn-off any man ever came across, and he'd find being dropped by her one big relief. She slipped her fingers inside his shirt and spread them against the rough warmth of his chest. 'Whatever the cause, this is a lovely way to start the day,' she said. That was the straightforward truth, anyway. 'Where are you staying?'

'You'll be able to see for yourself. I'll sneak you out there one evening—several evenings!—as many as we can manage. It's a holiday cottage we used to use when I was a kid. It's been rented out for years, but it fell empty very opportunely and I didn't go ahead with a re-let. It's about ten miles away. And now, unless you want me to become decidedly ungentlemanly, how about breakfast? I made sure there was coffee, and there are some rolls in the freezing compartment of the fridge that we can crisp up.'

'You think of everything, don't you?' Annabel surprised a look on his face that sent a sharp stab of excitement down into the pit of her stomach.

He lifted her off his knee and smacked her bottom, sending her in the direction of the bedroom. 'Right now what I'm thinking of would make that hair of yours curl even more wildly! So go and put more of a barrier between us, will you, while I make breakfast.'

Afterwards, the thought of the two of them having breakfast glowed like a jewel in her mind, a heady mixture of delight for all the senses. The smell of freshly ground coffee and crusty bread ... the dappled green light from the garden as though they were suspended at the very heart of nature ... Piers sitting opposite her, making her laugh, making her curl up inside at the things he said, the way his eyes glowed with warmth when he looked at her, the way his hand reached out for hers across the table.

Cutting through the memory, though, and with bitter poignancy, came the thought that had to be faced. It wasn't real. None of it was real. It was a make-believe relationship that she had created only to destroy it when the moment was ripe.

Remember that, she urged herself desperately. Remember it, or you'll destroy yourself instead of your enemy. A pang went through her at the word. Her *beloved* enemy . . .

She threw herself into her work with energy born of desperation. It was all right when she was working, her mind and body obeying one clear master. Surprisingly, it was all right when she was alone with Piers too, giving herself entirely to her purpose. She could even congratulate herself when a whirlwind of sensation swept through her. It meant she was doing a good job, didn't it? How could she enslave Piers' feelings if she remained totally unmoved herself? Even the jealousy she felt on the nights when Piers went casually off with Vivienne after the evening meal— that simply meant that she was playing her part right.

It was when she was alone that her duplicity closed in on her; accused her from all sides; threatened to crush her with shame. Those were the unbearable times. Fortunately there was no need to spend much time alone. There was always someone ready for a chat over coffee, a walk through the rolling fields and woodlands, a trip down to The Lamb.

So she got by . . . until the day when Piers came in to a rehearsal for the first time and her world blew up in her face.

It was the end of the afternoon and Annabel was perched

on a stool in front of the curtains with the other principals. Everything had been going well with the Friday rehearsal, until she saw someone slip into the back of the auditorium and sit down. He was in the shadows, but she knew at once that it was Piers.

For the first time her two worlds collided, creating wild confusion in her: the supposedly unreal world of the stage that for her offered the only reality, and the 'real' world of human relationships that for her was so crushingly false.

'Annabel?' She suddenly realised that the pianist had played her introduction and was pausing, looking across at her, puzzled because she had not come in.

'Sorry. I . . . Sorry.'

'Take it again.' Charles nodded to the pianist, raising his baton, and the notes of the introduction rang out a second time.

She opened her mouth, but nothing happened. No sound, no music, none of the liquid notes of love that should have poured out of her. Only a strangling pressure in her throat. Panic flared through her, and as the pianist faltered into silence again, she stared into Charles' eyes with dumb horror.

'What is it, Annabel?'

'I—I don't know.' Her voice was strained, croaking almost.

'Frog in your throat?'

'Don't say you've got a cold!' Vivienne slid her stool away noisily. 'For heaven's sake don't give it to me!'

'I haven't. It isn't.' Annabel's hand went up to her neck, and fear made her voice rise. 'What's the matter with me? There's nothing there. I can't sing!'

All their eyes were staring at her as she looked

desperately around. Beyond Charles she could see Piers walking at first slowly, then faster towards the front of the Opera House.

'You were thrown by missing your intro, I expect,' Charles said easily. 'Let's try again.'

She couldn't bear the thought of once more going through that worse-than-death emptiness of having no music in her.

'It's late, Charles.' Piers' voice, sounding calm and matter-of-fact, cut in. 'Don't you think you'd better call it a day? No point in overdoing it?'

Charles looked at his watch and nodded. 'Okay. We'll break for now, folks. Next rehearsal Monday, two o'clock sharp. On time, please, Vivienne. And preferably with voices!' He wiggled his eyebrows at Annabel.

There was a relieved burst of laughter and an outbreak of noise as people began getting music together and dropping stools back down into the orchestra pit.

Piers ran lightly up the steps and on to the stage where Annabel was standing, still frozen in fear. He picked up the music she seemed incapable of gathering together and then took her arm in his firm hand.

'Come on,' he said softly, as though there was no one else around. 'I think we need to talk.'

CHAPTER NINE

SOMEHOW Piers got her out of the Opera House and down to the lodge in his car. He took her shoulder bag from her and found the keys, almost carrying her inside when he had opened the door. He switched on both bars of the electric fire and pulled the settee up close to it, then sat rubbing her hands while she stared at the glowing bars like a zombie, her thoughts zooming in on her in a frightening spiral.

He was calm, solid, asking nothing until she began slowly to pull out of the cold fear that immobilised her, and his name was the first word she managed to speak.

'Piers . . .' Her eyes, huge, dark with shadows, turned at last to him.

'Feeling a bit better? Good.'

'Piers—I couldn't——' Annabel's teeth chattered as uncontrollable shivering shook her.

'Don't try to talk about it yet. I'm going to put the kettle on. Will you be all right?'

She nodded, hugging her arms round herself, and listened while the comforting sounds of water and teacups in the kitchen came as though from a great distance. She was beginning to feel warm again now, and if she stared hard enough at the twin red bars in front of her she could stop herself thinking.

'Here we are: strong and sweet, whether you want it like that or not.' He drew up a small table and put her cup in front of her. 'Take it as hot as you can manage.' He steadied

153

her hand while she drank, and when the cup was empty he began to talk as he refilled it. 'You know, I've seen this sort of thing happen before. There's nothing really wrong with your voice. I stood outside the doors listening for quite a while before I came in. You were on top form. You sounded marvellous.'

'But then ... nothing. I couldn't get a note out, Piers.' Her voice shook, didn't sound like her. 'What happened to me?'

'You had an attack of nerves. Something made your throat muscles close up on you.'

'What if it goes on happening? What if it happens in the middle of a performance? Oh, Piers, it was terrifying! Like being shut in somewhere, unable to get out.'

'It's never happened to you before?'

'No, never.' Her face looked so vulnerable, so afraid. He pulled her into his arms and held her, his hand stroking the back of her head, hypnotic and soothing.

'Don't be so frightened. We'll have a good talk about it, but not now. Right now I think you need to get away from here.'

Annabel looked up in increased alarm. 'I don't want to see anyone.' Not her parents, not her friends ... no one.

'You're not going to. Can you sling a few necessities into a bag? Warm clothes, toilet things, that's all? I'll do it for you if you can't.'

'I can manage.' She felt as though she was sleep-walking as she went into the bedroom, watching herself from somewhere just above her own head. Warm things, Piers had said. She looked blankly down into the drawer where her jumpers were kept, then pulled out a couple at random.

She was incapable of choice. Anything would do. She didn't even begin to wonder where he was taking her. She just wanted someone else to be in charge for a little while, someone else to do the thinking.

In the other room she could hear Piers using the phone, his voice brisk, concise, businesslike. Piers would take charge of everything. Sometimes it was the only thing to do . . . hand all decisions over to someone else . . . let yourself drift.

'Got everything? Toilet things, Your old blue dressing-gown?' She nodded, managing a faint smile at the mention of the last item.

'Right, I'll just dump these in the sink.' Piers was rapidly collecting the tea-things together, turning off the fire, going back into the bedroom to switch off the light she had left on, while she stood watching him in a stupor, her holdall in her hand.

'I've phoned the canteen to say you'll be away this weekend, and I've told Charles that I'm taking you home. He assumed it was your home, so I let him think that.'

She nodded slowly, asking nothing, and with a little smile he put an arm round her shoulders and shepherded her out to the car.

Lights were burning in the courtyard windows and up in the top floor flat where the warden lived in the main house as they passed. Deep in the trees beyond the lake, Vivienne's windows twinkled.

The Audi swept down the drive and Annabel settled down in her seat with a faint sigh of relief as they left everything behind.

'Warm enough? Comfortable?' asked Piers, looking down at her.

'Yes, thank you.'

He put his hand over hers. 'You'll be all right, believe me. We'll be there in twenty minutes.'

That meant they were going to the cottage. It was just a fact, neither pleasing nor disturbing. Piers was in charge, and Annabel closed her eyes for the rest of the journey.

Once inside the cottage with its worn, homely furnishings and its aromatic wood-burning stove, she felt to be slowly coming back to life.

'Supper first!' said Piers, taking her bag and putting it down. 'I wasn't expecting company, so it'll have to be something simple. I can take care of broccoli and cheese sauce if you can do us an omelette. Is that possible?'

'Yes! For goodness' sake, I'm not an invalid!'

'Glad to hear it!' He smiled appreciatively at the note of spirit that had crept into her voice, and she followed him out into the kitchen.

He had brought her to the cottage the previous week, and she knew where most things were. Quietly she got on with laying the table in the living-room, and when that was done started work on the omelette.

'How long before your bit's ready?' she asked, hesitating before pouring the whisked eggs into the pan.

'This is almost finished. I'm just waiting for the cheese sauce to thicken.' He glanced up at her. 'What are you smiling at?'

'You, slaving over a hot stove. It doesn't seem in character.'

'Really? I have a very wide range of skills, I'd have you know. Things you've never even dreamed of.' He gave her a wicked look, then went back to his cooking, managing to look as dangerously masculine in his navy and white striped plastic apron as he did at any other time. They worked silently side by side until the food was ready to be dished up, then carried their plates through into the living-room.

Piers put a cassette on while they ate: Mozart's 21st Piano Concerto. Annabel had felt a stirring of alarm when he went to the music centre. She couldn't have stood vocal music—not yet.

By the time she had finished her second glass of wine she felt less edgy, but her mind still bucked with fright when Piers said:

'I'll go and make some coffee, then we'll talk.'

She was glad he didn't look at her, and by the time he came back with a tray she was in shaky command of herself once again.

'Come and sit nearer the stove.' He stretched out a hand to lead her over to the settee and his fingers were warm and reassuring round hers. He kept her hand in his, pulling the table with their steaming cups on it within easy reach.

'I told you I'd seen something like what happened to you before, didn't I?' he began. 'She was young—about your age—and she'd married early and, it began to seem, a bit unwisely. The relationship was not very stable, and she'd got involved with someone else in the company she was working with. Her husband had no idea, because he never came to any of the shows she was in, claiming that he didn't like music. Then one night he turned up unexpectedly—got it into his head that his lack of interest was what was wrong. Someone told her he was there, and exactly the same thing happened as did to you. She couldn't get a note out. Someone had to do a quick costume change and go on in place of her.'

'But what's that to do with me? I'm not married. I'm not having an affair. How can someone else's problems and someone else's failure comfort me?' Annabel had edged forward in her agitation and Piers gently eased her back against the cushions.

'Not comfort, but maybe help to explain. You were perfectly all right until I came into the Opera House today, weren't you? The timing can't have escaped your notice. As soon as you were aware of me, you couldn't sing. Don't you see the similarity? Deception acting on the nerves? My coming in when you were singing brought the situation too close for comfort. Annabel, my love, you weren't made for it. You're an honest person, and being dishonest hits you hard where it matters most—in your voice. Do you understand?

Her heart was racing. He had no idea of the depths of deception in her. He was right—only he didn't know just how horribly right he was. She had a wild desire to pour out eveything there and then, but how could she? Apart from anything else, she was in a cottage miles from anywhere, and when she told Piers what she really thought of him— and worse when she revealed her true self—she wanted to be able to get away from him at once, and easily. The timing must be right, too. As long as they were thrown together at Temple Charing, things must stay as they were. She closed her eyes and swallowed hard.

'Well, do you understand?' he repeated. 'Do you see that once you've stopped all this secrecy about us, you won't have anything to worry about and there'll be no need for your psyche to play tricks on you?'

She turned and looked up into his face. 'I'm sure you're right, as usual.' Her smile softened the half-implied reproach. 'But I feel so tired, Piers—and still frightened. Is it cowardly of me not to want to talk about it any more tonight?'

His long, firm fingers gently traced the shape of her face, the curve of her neck. 'Probably quite sensible. You're suffering from reaction—you took quite a punishing blow tonight. Let me give you a brandy.'

'I'll fall asleep!' she protested.

He lowered his head and kissed her lips. 'That was the idea. The best thing for you. I've planted the explanation in your mind. Your subconscious can work on what to do about it without your direct help.'

He got up and fetched her a glass, its fine balloon shape cradling the amber liquid in its base.

'Maybe I'll take this up with me and drink it in bed.' Annabel stood up, then hesitated, realising she didn't know where to go.

'You can't get lost,' said Piers, picking up her holdall. 'There's only one bedroom up there.' Her eyes flew to meet his. 'But a perfectly adequate bed-settee down here.' He smiled and half pulled out the seat where they had been sitting to demonstrate. 'Don't worry, the only reason I'll come up is to use the bathroom and bring you a hot water bottle. Nothing else is on the agenda for tonight.'

The bedroom was tiny, its roof sloping towards a diamond-paned dormer window, and there wasn't much room for anything: just the bed, a pine wardrobe, one chair and a chest of drawers with brass handles that matched the wardrobe.

Annabel took her nightdress and dressing-gown and went across the tiny landing to the bathroom, where, after the sketchiest of baths and cleaning her teeth, she picked up her day clothes in an untidy bundle and went back to the bedroom.

The curtains were drawn, the lamp on the chest lit, and Piers was straightening up after putting the bottle in bed. He smiled at her.

'You look like a tired twelve-year-old!'

'I feel like it.' She dropped her clothes on the chair and stood there, feeling very miserable and lost.

'Come here!' He pulled her towards him, slipping his arms inside the loosely hanging front of her dressing-gown, so that she could feel his warmth and strength through the thin cotton of her nightdress.

The little room with its white walls, pink-shadowed now from the glow of the lamp, seemed to close in protectively round the two of them. Annabel felt the core of fear inside her melt away into the warmth of Piers' embrace. The world distanced itself. Tomorrow was light-years away. There was only now, only Piers' mouth, gentle, loving, on hers.

It was against all reason, against logic, against everything. But it was what she needed. Just the two of them so close that nothing could intrude on their private world. No past to cast its shadow on them, no future to threaten.

His lips moved gently over her face, kissed her closed eyes.

'You'd better get into bed, love. For a million reasons,' he said softly, then the safe private world was beginning to disintegrate. She caught his hand and clung to it.

'I don't want you to go—not yet.'

'Then I won't, but get into bed. It's cold.' He sat on the edge, his arm round her, waiting while she sipped the brandy, grimacing owlishly at its strength.

'It feels to be lighting up my inside!'

His fingers squeezed her shoulder. 'Then it'll be all the more effective. Finished?' He took the glass from her and put it down, and she slid down into the warm bed. Piers turned the chair to face her and moved to sit on it, and she reached again for his hand, cradling it in hers, pressed against her cheek on the soft pillow.

She felt him turn round to switch off the lamp, then there was only the shaft of light from the landing falling across the floor as her eyelids closed. She rubbed her face sleepily in the palm of his hand, her mind muzzing over with sleep. Piers was here with her. She was safe. She felt his other hand on her hair, his fingers slipping thought its silkiness, smoothing it away from her temples with soothing rhythm, his warm breath gently fanning her skin. She could relax now. Nothing could hurt her.

She must have slept like a log, but when she woke with light glimmering round the edges of the curtains, both Piers and the illusion of safety had gone. What was she doing here? Why had she behaved so illogically last night? How could she have imagined there was any safety with the man who was at the root of everything that worried her?

The bedroom seemed suddenly a prison. She had to get out . . . clear her thoughts before she saw Piers this morning and he began to work his crazy magic on her mind again. She pulled on her clothes, adding an extra jumper from the bag. It was cold enough in the bedroom; it would be worse out of doors.

She trod gingerly on the very side of the stairs on the way down, scared of making a noise with every movement. Her coat was on a hook behind the door. She lifted it down and shrugged her arms into its cold sleeves. The door into the living-room was slightly ajar, and she peeped heart-in-mouth through the gap. Piers was a dark head and a bare brown shoulder over the bedclothes on the settee, his back towards her, still apparently asleep.

Annabel relaxed a bit and cautiously turned the key, freezing again when the lock clicked sharply into the 'open' position. There was a sudden stirring from the living-room and a deep, sleepy voice called out.

'Annabel?'

She fled out, closing the door behind her and running down the path before she realised she was heading into a wall of whiteness.

Fog—November fog—but it didn't matter. Maybe it was only patchy and she would walk out of it in no time. She turned right out of the gate, the way they had come in last night, and walked briskly through the cloudy whiteness, past hedges pearled with moisture and grass heavy and beaded at the side of the road. It was quiet, utterly quiet, and the fog came with her, muffling her footsteps, closing behind her so that she could see neither where she was going nor where she had come from. The hedge continued unbroken except by the occasional gate into a field, but she had known that there were no other houses near, and she wanted none. Just time to think.

She was half-way over a crossroads before she realised it, with four vague openings disappearing into obscurity. She hesitated, wondering which direction to take, and suddenly realised that the throbbing sound of a vehicle was approaching, seeming to be all round her. Where was it coming from? She spun round, peering through the wavering whiteness, until suddenly through the gloom

twin yellow spheres broke out, growing larger and brighter
with what seemed like alarming speed.

Annabel flew to the side and leaned back into the hedge
while the car, an old Morris, square and prim, chugged
past, its driver hunched over the wheel, eyes glued to the
road, totally unaware of her presence.

The sound of its engine died away into silence and the
fog settled in again as she stepped out from the hedge,
brushing down her coat where the brown leaves clung to it.
The only sensible thing was to go back. She couldn't think
in these conditions.

She took a few steps forward, then stopped. Which road
had she come from? She had turned round looking for the
car, and then flown to the side—any side for safety—and
now she had no idea of the way back to the cottage.

All you have to do, she told herself, is walk a little way in
each direction and you'll hit the cottage eventually. She
began to do this, but the fog made distance hard to judge.
Was this one of the gates she had passed on her way to the
crossroads? No, she had been walking on the other side. She
retraced her steps, walking more quickly as she began to
feel claustrophobic in the smothering whiteness, breathing
more quickly and coughing as the fog caught at her throat.

You fool! she told herself. If you really want to be unable
to sing, this is the best way to go about it. Back at the
crossroads she made herself stand still and control her
breathing. It was then that she heard quick footsteps and
saw a tall shape emerging from the dimness across the road.
Piers! Once again he represented safety, and she rushed to
him, only to have her shoulders roughly seized and shaken.

'You little idiot! What madness sent you out in this stuff?'
he said harshly. He had drops of moisture beading his

eyebrows and clinging to his hair, and he was angry—so angry that the whole shape of his face had sharpened into an almost vulpine angularity.

He took her arm, gripping it just above the elbow, and began to march her back the way he had come. 'Is there no end to all the nonsense? Is this how it's always going to be with you—one drama after another? Last night I thought you were beginning to see sense. This morning, for some inexplicable reason, you risk life, limb and voice in this stuff!'

'I only wanted a walk.' Annabel's voice bounced as she broke into a little run to keep up with him.

He gave her arm a shake. 'A walk! Didn't you hear me call you? Couldn't you have changed your mind when you saw what it was like out of doors?'

She tucked her face down inside her collar, judging silence the prudent course.

Back at the cottage he slammed the door shut and followed her into the living-room. 'I'd like to put you over my knee and beat some sense into you!' he said angrily, pulling her round to face him.

Instead he kissed her—a very different matter from the tenderness of last night. This was the Bellingham she had first judged him to be—bruising, dominant, demanding.

She tugged away, rubbing her mouth. 'Nobody kisses me like that!'

'I do. Shut up. Sit down.' She was so taken aback by his tone that she obeyed. 'I've had enough of this,' he went on, striding to and fro in front of her. 'I'm not renowned for my patience. I'm a man who usually gets what he wants with a minimum of delay. For some reason *you*——' he stabbed a sharp finger at her '—*you* have turned me into something different. Well, it's not going on, because that way trouble seems to lie—dead trouble. I'll tell you what you're going to do.' He stopped moving suddenly and stood glaring at her. 'You're going to forget all this nonsense about keeping things dark. You're going to forget your damned pride and the possibility that a fraction of your glory might be held back from you. You're going to marry me as quickly as we can arrange it—and then you'll be able to sing your ruddy heart out!'

She sat staring at him, and a strange calmness and stillness fell on her. He had given her the solution. In that one short outburst he had offered her a speeding towards the inevitable end, presenting her with the most crushing setting for her rejection of him: a wedding day. He had made the way ahead clear, just as he had made her way back to the cottage clear.

She knew too that she was going to have to leave Temple Charing. It was unthinkable that she should stay on with people who knew him, in a setting where she was likely, however infrequently, to have to see him again. She would go back to Doug Ryman and get herself some work of some kind—not as good, of course, but with a millionth part of the complications she had lived through since she reluctantly threw in her lot with Piers Bellingham.

'Well?' he barked at her. 'Say something, damn you!'

'Yes, Piers.' Her voice was soft and steady. 'I'll agree to a wedding whenever you like.'

He stared at her with almost comic disbelief, and subsided before her eyes. 'The devil you will!' he said slowly, then rallied. 'Get on the phone to your parents now. Tell them we're coming over to see them this morning.'

Even that didn't throw her. It was as though all the answers were there.

'No—please. If we tell them they'll insist on a proper wedding with heaven knows how much delay. And they'll feel they have to incur loads of expense they just can't afford. Let's just do it, then tell them afterwards. It's my only condition, Piers. Promise me you'll tell no one. Let it be just us.'

He hesitated, but she didn't worry. She knew what his answer would be, however long he trembled on a knife-edge, and it was no surprise when he held out his arms to her. 'All right. If you're sure that's what you want—anything, so long as we put an end to all this trouble. Just us,' he said.

A week later—a strange, dreamlike week—Annabel stood at the window of the Russell Square hotel where she had spent the night, waiting for the telephone to ring with the message that the taxi ordered to take her to the register office had arrived.

Piers had spent much of the week in London and out and about in the Midlands, and he had not come near the Opera House during rehearsals, so there had been no further trouble with her singing. In fact, she had never sung better, knowledge that this was the only brief time she would have with the company adding poignancy and depth to the sadness her leading role demanded.

She allowed herself no feelings of guilt at the thought of leaving Temple Charing. They would soon find someone else. No one was irreplaceable.

The secret times she spent with Piers had been a strain, like a role she hadn't managed to think herself properly into. She was supposed to be a bride-to-be, but there was no conviction in her behaviour, only a brittle gaiety that rang falsely in her own ears. What Piers had made of it, she had no idea. She had caught him looking at her in a strangely contemplative way once or twice, but he had probably put it all down to the same strain that had silenced her voice only a week ago.

Last night had been the hardest of all: a romantic dinner for two that she approached with feelings more appropriate to a wake. She had talked non-stop. What on earth had she said? There was no memory of the words or of the dancing she had flung herself into—only the doom-like sense of moving towards something horrific.

'It's nearly over ...' Piers had said tenderly when he kissed her goodnight, and she had been forced to run away from him before the depth of meaning the three words had for her spilled over in visible anguish.

She tried now to imagine Piers getting ready for the ceremony he thought would be taking place in half an hour's time, and coldness gathered at the pit of her stomach.

The phone trilled, startling her, although she was expecting it.

'Your taxi, Miss Foley.'

'Thank you. I'll be right down.' Annabel picked up her case and gave a last look round before closing the bedroom door and making for the lift. She had that strange feeling of being outside herself again, a spectator of events in which her body was taking part.

She told the driver the name of the register office as she got in the cab, and he looked at her jeans and pink sweater with mild interest.

'Going to watch the famous getting hitched, are you?'

'No, just meeting someone with a message. I shall want you to wait for me and take me on to Paddington afterwards.'

She checked the contents of her shoulder bag nervously. The envelope for Piers was there, and her resignation had been posted to Temple Charing early that morning. Would there be trouble over her broken contract? She didn't imagine so. It wouldn't be in Piers' interest to have much discussion as to why she had gone. He would give some pseudo-medical reason—nervous exhaustion, maybe. Wasn't that the term they used to describe behaviour that seemed irrational?

She certainly felt exhausted. She had not gone down for breakfast that morning ... hadn't felt able to eat a thing. And now she was sick and trembling as the London streets flashed by.

'Nearly there,' said the taxi-driver. 'You want me to keep her ticking over? I shan't be able to wait long.'

'It won't be necessary. I shall be very quick.'

He was slowing down, and her heart gave a sickening lurch as she saw Piers standing there at the side of the doorway, elegant in a pale grey suit, his dark head turning towards her as the taxi drew up.

He saw her through the window, and a smile lit up his face, then, as she opened the door and stepped out on to the pavement, she saw the smile freeze and fade, saw him look at her jeans and sweater, then seek her own eyes in sharp alarm.

The sense of living in a dream that had carried her through the week drained away. This was real. It was happening. *She* was making it happen. And oh, it was unbearable!

She began to move towards him, incapable of tearing her eyes from his, unsure with each step whether her legs would go on supporting her. And he stood there with a frightening stillness, waiting for her to come to him.

When she was close enough, she stopped and fixed her eyes on the white carnation in his buttonhole. There was one silver droplet of water on its central petals like a tear, a drop that seemed to enlarge and shrink alternately as she stared at it.

'I'm not marrying you—I never intended to. Right from the start it was all pretence. Kate Elston was my friend. She was happy, and you destroyed her. She wrote from your house: "Piers says he will never marry me". That was what she said, and she was sick, heartbroken enough to die because of you.' Annabel took a trembling breath. 'Now *you* know how it feels to be discarded as you discarded Kate. Here's your locket.'

She thrust the envelope at him, and only then did she look up into his face again. He was staring at her, and he was still ... so very still. His eyes were narrow, dark, unreadable.

'So that's what it's all been about . . .' he said slowly, and of all the words she could have imagined these were the flattest. Then his hand went to his lapel to pull the carnation from his buttonhole, and as he dropped the flower on the pavement, the drop of moisture from its heart splashed on to Annabel's hand, searing it like burning metal.

It was all wrong. *He* was icily calm. *She*, who had intended to hurt him, felt to be destroying herself.

She turned blindly and made for the taxi, Piers' eyes burning into her back as she ran, and it felt as though

invisible chains binding her to him were tearing the heart
out of her. As she groped for the door handle she heard him
call her name, his voice harsh and peremptory.

'Annabel!'

She stumbled into the cab. 'Go! For God's sake, go!' she
choked.

CHAPTER TEN

THE TAXI driver insisted on carrying Annabel's cases to the train.

'I'll tell you straight,' he said with brusque concern before he left her on the platform, 'I've been mixed up in some funny things in my time, but this takes some beating. Are you going to be all right? You sure?'

'Yes, thank you.' Annabel answered like a child who has had lessons in politeness. She hadn't allowed herself to cry. Why cry when Piers felt nothing?

The ticket collector and an elderly lady on the train asked if she was all right too, and she gave them the same polite, cool little answer. Why did people keep speaking to her like that? She was sitting perfectly quietly on her seat, wasn't she? She was looking straight ahead, not staring at anybody, so why should they all keep peering into her face, speaking to her as though she were slightly deaf, or not quite right in the head?

Where was she going? She sat forward on the edge of the seat, frowning in concentration. Going away . . . going away . . . going away . . . the train wheels rattled. But away where? Oh yes—Cheltenham, where she had put her things from Temple Charing in the left luggage office. She sank back into the fixed, white-faced stare again.

And after Cheltenham? The question dropped into her mind at the end of another period of blankness. Somewhere to sleep. Somewhere to shut out all the people who stared and whispered to each other and asked if she was all right when of course she was perfectly all right.

At Cheltenham, weighed down by two heavy cases, she had the most frightening narrow escape. Suddenly she saw Charles coming towards her with Hugh, hurrying in the direction of the trains. They were deep in discussion with each other, and she was able to slip into a cloakroom before they saw her, but she was so shattered that she stayed there for an endless time, knowing that she couldn't risk spending the night in that town and maybe bumping into someone else she knew who would want to talk and ask questions.

What had happened to her thinking capacity? She couldn't concentrate. She kept staring at the grubby wooden floorboards in the waiting room, going off into a trance until she realised that someone else was looking oddly at her again.

Doug Ryman—the name slipped into her mind and she seized on it. Yes, of course, that was where she must go. See Doug, ask him to take her back on his books. That was what she should have done originally, instead of—— But she didn't want to think of the direction her life had taken since she last saw Doug. Those thoughts shimmered and danced dangerously in her mind. They were to be avoided.

There was a long wait before the Birmingham train. Somehow most of the afternoon had gone by and lights were glowing all over the station and flashing from the windows of the trains that rattled through as she sat on the cold platform. Eventually her train was announced and she managed to get herself and her cases on to it.

Before the departure time a wedding party came dashing along the platform, and Annabel's breathing quickened. She didn't want the bride and groom to come into her compartment. There was some reason why it would be very wrong indeed for them to come near her with their laughter and confetti spilling from their hair and clothes.

They ran on down the platform, and it was a great relief.

At the end of the journey, the Holiday Inn was the only Birmingham hotel she could think of to tell the taxi driver, its name bitterly inappropriate to the way she felt. It would be expensive too, and she couldn't go on affording it, but just for tonight, and maybe tomorrow, she would indulge herself. There was some reason why she felt in need of pampering, but she wouldn't let herself think of it now.

Later, in the anonymous comfort of the hotel bedroom, she had a hot bath and crawled into bed, falling at once into a numb, leaden sleep until just before dawn.

It was then, in the cold beginning of another day, that she let herself remember just how alone she was, just how directionless her future, and she cried until she was exhausted enough to sleep again.

The room maid woke her mid-morning when she let herself in to make the bed.

'Sorry, madam,' she apologised. 'I had no idea anyone was still in the room. Are you all right?'

That question again.

'One-day 'flu, I think,' Annabel improvised wearily. 'I'd like to stay put. I'll ring down to reception and tell them I'll be here for one more night. Just ignore the room, will you? I don't want it cleaned.'

'Would you like anything sent up? A light meal maybe?'

'No, nothing, thank you.' Annabel turned away, pulling up the clothes. The thought of food was unbearable, and she had tea and coffee-making equipment in the room if she wanted either.

'Well, if you're sure . . .' The woman hovered undecidedly a moment, then went away, closing the door gently behind her.

The hours of Sunday ticked slowly by, time having no meaning in the grey twilight of Annabel's mind. By evening she was beginning to pull herself together, and got out of bed long enough to look out clothes for the following day and hang them in the steam of the bathroom for the creases to drop out while she had a bath and washed her hair.

The sight of her face in the mirror explained the questions directed at her. She was deathly white, her eyes huge, with shadows in their depths as well as underneath them. Tomorrow she would put on plenty of make-up. She wasn't going back to Doug looking like a wounded animal. If only her hand would stop going up to her neck where the locket used to be . . .

Not surprisingly she woke early on Monday morning and went as far as ordering a continental breakfast in the dining-room, but the sounds of life around her seemed so loud and harsh after her isolation that she didn't even attempt to eat, only drank a cup of black coffee before going back to her room.

At nine she rang Doug's secretary and was given an appointment for eleven o'clock without any difficulty. After she had seen Doug, it would soon be time for the lunchtime edition of the *Evening Mail*. There would be accommodation to look at, and Doug would surely let her leave her cases with him while she went to find somewhere possible to live.

This time the taxi driver dumped her cases on the pavement and left her to struggle with them herself, a tribute to the time she had spent assisting nature in front of the Holiday Inn's mirror. She left them one on top of the other in the lobby at the foot of the stairs leading to Doug's office. If they were stolen, that was that. She couldn't wrestle them up the stairs.

The secretary was different—blonde, and younger, and the office had been repainted. Things seemed to be looking up for Doug. A good sign?

'Miss Foley?' The girl eyed Annabel and her mulberry dress and white jacket with interest. 'Oh, yes, he's expecting you. Just one moment, and I'll tell him you're here.' She got up and opened the inner door. 'Your eleven o'clock appointment, Mr Ryman.'

Doug's voice, rough and warm as ever, rang out. 'Right, Tracey, ask her to come in, will you?'

He came to the door to meet Annabel, shaking her hand with crushing enthusiasm. 'Hello there, doll! What's all this, then? Come on in and sit down.'

'Hello, Doug. Thanks for seeing me.'

He stood back to let her enter, and she was past him and halfway towards the desk before she saw the tall figure standing by the window, the dark, set face staring at her. It was Piers . . . and he was stepping towards her, his eyes cold as winter.

'*No!*' Annabel's precarious calm deserted her and she spun round to fly from the room.

Doug's face creased in a half-ashamed grimace as he blocked her exit. 'Sorry, doll!' He closed the door in her face, and when she groped for the handle to let herself out, Piers' hand came down on hers, pulling her away and round to face him. With his free hand he turned the key in the lock, slipping it into his pocket.

'Not the same trick twice running, Annabel,' he said coldly. 'This time you'll stay put a little longer.'

'I don't want to talk.' She was trembling from head to foot.

'Possibly not—but I've got a lot to say to you.'

She had just time to register that he was looking more sharply at her, then his face seemed to be coming and going, disappearing into blackness, and she needed to direct all her concentration towards remaining upright.

She felt his hands on her arms, and for a moment she was tempted to let herself fall forward against the strong support of his chest.

'Come over here to the chair. Steady does it.' His voice was a long way off—or maybe it was because suddenly there seemed to be trains rushing through the office ... electric trains with a high-pitched sound, blocking out the light from the window.

'Put your head down.' She felt his hand on her back, bending her over until her head touched her knees and she could see his shining black shoes swelling and shrinking alarmingly like something in a distorting mirror at a fairground. She closed her eyes to shut them out, and struggled to still the world as it whirled round her.

Piers was speaking to someone, but she couldn't follow what he was saying. Then he was back by her side, his hand on her shoulder.

'Stay like that until your head clears,' he ordered.

She was aware of him moving to sit on the edge of the desk, and gradually things slowed down to a standstill. Gingerly she raised her head, putting up her hand to feel moisture beading her forehead and looking at her fingers in bewilderment.

'Here.' He pushed a folded handkerchief into her hand and slowly she wiped her face and hands, then closed her eyes again.

'When did you last eat?'

Annabel thought back with difficulty.

'Yesterday? Saturday?' he prompted.

'I've had drinks,' she said lamely.

'That meal you played around with on Friday? That was the last one?' Piers asked incredulously. She nodded, still not opening her eyes. 'You little fool!' he said softly.

The door opened. So he had unlocked it—not that it made any difference. She wasn't feeling like moving.

'Thanks, Tracey. Put it down here.' High heels tapped across the floor, the door closed again, and there was the sound of liquid being poured and a spoon stirring, then a cup was put in her hands. 'Drink that, and when you've finished, eat these. Don't be silly!' He brushed aside her protesting hand and dropped a couple of biscuits in her lap.

The tea was strong and sweet, and though she hated sugar she drank it greedily. She ate the biscuits too, swallowing them with more difficulty, but persevering because somehow she had to find the strength to walk out of there. The silence was beginning to weigh heavily.

'Why are you in Birmingham?' she asked, when it seemed as though he was never going to speak.

'Isn't that obvious? The most hardened criminal has right of reply.' She could picture his expression without seeing it. Cold, accusing, hating her.

'But you didn't know I was going to be here.'

'It only took a simple process of elimination. You hadn't gone back to Russell Square. You weren't at Marta's. You weren't back at the lodge. You weren't at your parents'——'

Her eyes flew wide open then, horrified. 'You didn't tell *them*? Oh, how could you? They had no idea.'

'And still haven't. For your information, I was a college friend ringing to ask for a forwarding address. If you'd been there they would have said so. As it was, they gave me the Temple Charing address, so it was obvious they knew nothing.'

Annabel swallowed hard. 'Nobody knows. Only me.'

'Only stupid, idiotic you!'

She put the cup down with an alarming rattle. 'I realise that you're angry, but I'm not going to sit here and be insulted. I'm not sorry for what I did.' Unthinkingly she let herself look at Piers again, and the sight of his face made her heart clench in remorse. Not sorry . . . just heartbroken. She attempted to get up and found herself back in her chair again, rudely pushed down by his hand.

'You'll go when I say so. I haven't finished yet.'

'But *I've* finished!' Her voice was shrill at the humiliation of her position. 'I've finished with you. Finished with Temple Charing. I wrote to them to say so.'

'I know you did. Here's the letter.' He felt in his pocket and slapped her letter to Charles on the desk in front of her, unopened. She stared from it to his cold, angry face.

'How did you get that?'

'I guessed you'd have written it, so I got to Temple Charing before the postman did.'

'You were wasting your time. It's not going to affect anything.'

He ignored her words. 'Then, guessing that Doug would be your next step, I phoned his flat and got him out of bed to

promise he'd let me know the minute he heard from you—
which accounts for the fact that I didn't have to break too
many speed limits to get here before you did.'

'I can't think why you did it. You—you didn't seem to
care at all when I told you on Saturday. I suppose you
thought I'd got off too lightly.'

His mouth mocked her. 'Pride again, Annabel? I'll
correct your choice of word. I wasn't *surprised* when you told
me.'

She stared at him in shock, and as he looked down into
her big grey eyes for the first time, the hard lines on his face
softened a little.

'Oh, Annabel! Did you think I knew you so little that I'd
be taken in by that sudden capitulation of yours at the
cottage? That volte-face that was as uncharacteristic of you
as anything could be? Oh, admittedly I couldn't quite work
out what you were up to, but I sure as hell knew you were
up to something. It stood out a mile. Someone with your
basic honesty can't lie about the things that matter. For the
past week you've been as brittle as ice. And as for the "secret
wedding" idea——' Piers sceptical expression left her in no
doubt of the failure of that particular ploy '—I've met your
family, remember. No way would you contemplate
depriving them of being at their only daughter's wedding.
The only surprising element in the whole business is that
you let things go so far before showing your hand. Did you
spend much time planning that scene for effect, tell me?
Did you ever consider letting it go on until we were
standing in front of the Registrar? Don't you feel you
sacrificed a bit of drama there?"

'Oh, stop! Please stop!' Annabel broke into the rising
tempo of his tirade with a choking plea. 'Why did you let

me go on if you were so clever?'

Piers turned away for a moment and from the movement of his jaw she knew he was making an attempt to control his anger. 'I've told you, I couldn't work out what you were up to. At first I thought you were playing for time, doing a fine balancing act between my impatience, your own undoubted distress over *something*, and your damned independent wish to do it *your* way. I couldn't believe you would let it go so far—and when we got to the actual day I really began to think I'd imagined it all, until I saw you get out of that taxi in your scruffy jeans. Nice touch, that, Annabel.' His voice was very bitter, and she remembered the carnation. Was it still lying there, crushed by hundreds of passing feet, unrecognisable?

He went on, 'Never in a million years, though, would I have hit on the real reason for your behaviour, believed you capable of stringing me along to such a point—and all because you felt enough hatred for me to believe a story that wouldn't stand up in a tuppenny romance.'

Hatred . . . Annabel's eyes swam with tears at the irony of his words. Oh, she had started out hating him, but the closer she came to the end, the more the knife had seemed to turn towards herself. And now it was there in her breast, hard, and ice-cold.

She opened her mouth to speak, but he made an impatient gesture and she shrank back involuntarily. 'Can you stand now? Are you fit to walk?'

'I'm not going anywhere. I'm here to see Doug.'

'This comes first. We've taken enough of Doug's time. We can't keep him out of his office any longer, and I've still got a lot to say to you. You're going to give me a hearing whether you like it or not, Annabel. And then you can do what you damned well like.'

Doug's secretary began typing rather too late as they walked through the reception area, and there was no sign of Doug.

'Thank Mr Ryman for the use of his office, will you, Tracey? And tell him I'll be in touch.' Piers spoke as though the situation were as normal as a routine business call, then he took Annabel's arm and steered her towards the door.

She could feel the girl's eyes on them in barely concealed interest as they left, and the typing stopped the minute they were beyond the door.

Somehow Piers managed to shuffle one of her cases up under his arm and pick up the second with the same hand, all without letting go of her. His car was a hundred yards or so down the road, and they covered the distance in a grim silence.

He started up the engine, and in minutes they were parking in the square by Gino's, but it was towards the garden that he directed her.

'This is the only place I could think of where we might get a bit of peace,' he explained. 'Come on, a bit of fresh air will do you good. And the place is public enough to make me moderate my behaviour.'

Dumbly, Annabel walked by his side into the garden, deserted now in the pre-lunch hour, with only city pigeons pecking away in the grass, turning over the fallen leaves in their hunt for food.

Piers waited until they had walked completely round the paths once before he began speaking again.

'What I can't understand is why you went so far on mere supposition,' he said. 'Why didn't you check your facts before putting us both through such a painful experience—

because I'm under no misapprehension that you didn't hurt yourself in the process, Annabel. I remember that time in the Opera House only too well—and afterwards. You can't fake something like that.'

'I did try to check my facts with you!' He would never know how much she had wanted him to explain her suspicions away. 'But I had Kate's letter written on paper from *your* house, remember . . . and on top of that there was your silence. You condemned yourself by refusing point blank to tell me what happened between her and you, Piers. You can't blame me. It all added up.'

'It added up to what you wanted it to add up to,' he said bitterly.

'No!' The word burst from her. 'I didn't want it to be like that. I——'

She stopped, choked by the feelings rising up in her.

'Yes?' They were standing staring at each other, her face flushed now after its earlier paleness, Piers' eyes intense, questioning. 'Go on. What were you going to say?'

There was only room for truth now. At least the dignity of that would colour this final parting.

'I wanted to believe you cared about me, that you weren't amusing yourself as you did with Kate,' she went on unsteadily. 'I even began to believe it, until I found that letter of hers with your address on it, and knew that she'd been living with you. I hated you then . . .' Her voice went low, so low that he could barely hear her. 'Or thought I did . . . I made up my mind that I would make you suffer as you had made Kate suffer. That was the night I came to your house, the night you gave me the locket.' Her hand went up to her neck, then finding nothing there, plucked nervously at the collar of her jacket. 'Hating you got harder and harder. There were times when I forgot about Kate. And the worst times of all when I remembered, and wanted to forget.' She raised her eyes to his, but she was too blinded by emotion to see his expression. 'If I'd done that—deliberately pushed Kate out of my mind and married the man who was so involved in her death—what would that have made me?'

Piers breathed in sharply as though about to speak, then stopped and felt her hands. 'You're cold.'

She shook her head and dashed away the tears from her eyes.

'Come and sit down while I do something I should have done ages ago. In a way, I've been as ridiculous as you—yes, ridiculous. What else can you call two people who champion someone who has no chance of benefiting from their actions, and pile up a whole load of unhappiness for themselves in the process?'

He found a seat in a recess facing the late November sun, surrounded on three sides by laurel hedges that cut out the wind, and when they were settled he began again.

'You seem to have thought of life in terms of grand opera, Annabel, and it's a much more humdrum affair. It consists of people who make mistakes, plans that fail, and unplanned things that suddenly happen. Real life isn't over-full of out-and-out villains. Nobody strung Kate along, nobody deceived her. She deceived herself. And the person who would "never marry her" wasn't me . . . it was Jerry King.'

'Jerry King?' Annabel repeated the pop singer's name in slow disbelief. 'Kate was involved with Jerry King?' She had seen him on television—at college once—but never would she have connected Kate with a man like him. He was wild. He had been up on more than one drugs charge, and his sex life was constant game for the tabloids.

'Yes. She met him in the early days in London, and really fell hard for him. It was all kept very quiet—didn't suit his image to have a girl-friend in tow. He had to be the ever-available idol. The only reason I found out was that I could never get in touch with her when I needed to, and we had an almighty row which culminated in her telling me what was going on. I warned her what she was getting into, of course, but it was no use. He promised her nothing—made no bones about the fact that he wasn't into permanent relationships—but she didn't believe him either. She was going to be the different one, the one who made him change. It was so sad . . . her belief in something that existed only in her own imagination. The inevitable happened, of course, and instead of changing him, she began to get involved in his way of life. She managed her stage commitments—but only just. Her health was obviously suffering from days of hard work and nights of God knows what. There was a lot of drinking going on . . . and then she was talked—or maybe tricked—into trying drugs. She had what Jerry King described as "a bad trip, man, that's all" . . . and it was the shock of that that made her finally realise that she had to get away from him and his crowd.

'I brought her to my home to give her a chance to recover in private. The drugs weren't a problem—she hadn't got deep enough in for that—but the combination of shock, exhaustion, and sheer let-down had brought her danger-ously low. I took her out of the show she was rehearsing, and cancelled everything until after Christmas, but she was restless. She wanted to drive herself on, to compensate for lost time. The day the accident happened she must have taken it into her head to try to get to a rehearsal in town, and she just wasn't up to it. It was a pure accident, Annabel. She didn't want to die—I *know* that. She was just too eager to get on with living.'

'Oh, poor Kate! Poor, poor Kate!' For a moment the tragedy and waste filled Annabel's mind to the exclusion of everything else. It was only as Piers continued that the enormity of her misjudgment began to take precedence.

'Afterwards,' he went on, 'it seemed that the only thing I could do was keep her private life private. Nobody else knew. There was speculation, of course—there always is in stage circles, but you know that. I stamped on it all as I did on your questions—misguidedly, if only I'd known.'

'Oh, Piers! I'm so ashamed.' Devastated now by the memory of her behaviour, Annabel turned to face him. 'There's nothing I can say, is there? To apologise for what I thought is so far from enough. It could *never* be enough.'

He looked steadily back at her, his dark eyes unfathomable. 'No, not enough in itself. But there are things you can do, starting with this.' He put the letter to Charles in her hands. 'Go on, tear it up. Come back to your senses.'

She looked down at the envelope and all it represented. A second chance, but at such a cost. How could she go on, seeing Piers as she inevitably would, knowing what she had thrown away through her own foolishness? How unbearably hollow such success would be!

'Your rehearsal is at two,' he said softly, 'and you know how much Charles dislikes latecomers. Your voice is a gift, Annabel. You can't treat it carelessly. Come back to Temple Charing.'

Annabel gave a shuddering sigh. She couldn't do it. After all that had happened, a clean break was the only possible course. A sadder, wiser beginning elsewhere.

'Come back to *me*,' Piers said then. Incredibly, astonishingly, those were the words he said.

She stared at him, not daring to believe what she had heard. Then, as she read in his eyes the truth of his feelings, her face crumpled.

'How could you possibly want me after what I've done?' she cried passionately. 'How could you ever forget it? It isn't possible? It——' His face had softened into a smile of heart-stopping warmth and his fingers came up to rest gently on her lips, silencing her.

'You gave me the answer to that yourself when you said you loved me in spite of what you imagined I'd done. The way I feel about you doesn't switch on and off, either, Annabel. It's there always. I came after you, didn't I? And if necessary I'll come after you to the ends of the earth.'

She gave a choked little sob and clung to him while her heart soared with unbelievable happiness. He held her close, and now, as they kissed, there was no shadow between them, no echo hanging in the air, nothing but the joy of their love uniting them totally.

'Could you *really* not hold it against me on our wedding day when you think of last time?' Annabel asked him moments later, still not daring to believe in her own happiness.

'Easily,' he said. 'For one thing, I imagine our real wedding will be totally different from the one that was never intended. It will be in a church you know, and where you're known, for instance.'

'With all the family there——'

'And friends——'

'Every one of them!'

'And the bride will most definitely not wear jeans!'

'Oh, Piers!' Annabel flung her arms round his neck again.

'There is one minor condition . . .' he began slowly.

'Yes?' Apprehensively she drew back to look into his face.

'You go over to that phone box——' he pointed to the side of the square '—and ring your parents this very moment, in my hearing.'

Annabel smiled radiantly at him. 'And Marta. We must tell Marta too. Come on! Hurry!'

She sprang to her feet and held out her hands.

Piers gave a quiet smile of satisfaction as he got up and folded her hands in the strength and warmth of his.

'Now I really believe you!' he said.

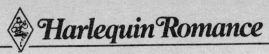

Harlequin Romance

Coming Next Month

Available in January wherever paperback books are sold, or through Harlequin Reader Service.

In the U.S.
901 Fuhrmann Blvd.
P.O. Box 1397
Buffalo, N.Y. 14240-1397

In Canada
P.O. Box 603
Fort Erie, Ontario
L2A 5X3

**For the millions who can't read
Give the Gift of Literacy**

One out of five adults in North America
cannot read or write well enough
to fill out a job application
or understand the directions on a bottle of medicine.

**You can change all this by joining the fight
against illiteracy.**

For more information write to:
Contact, Box 81826, Lincoln, Neb. 68501
In the United States, call toll free: 1-800-228-8813

**The only degree you need
is a degree of caring**

"This ad made possible with the cooperation of the Coalition for Literacy and the Ad Council."
Give the Gift of Literacy Campaign is a project of the book and periodical industry,
in partnership with Telephone Pioneers of America.

**He could torment her days with doubts
and her nights with desires that fired her soul.**

VITA VENDRESHA

He was everything she ever wanted. But they were opponents in
a labor dispute, each fighting to win. Would she risk her brilliant
career for the promise of love?